A RESURRECTION CHRONICLES NOVELLA

DEMON SHOCK

Also by M.J. Haag

Fairy Tale Retellings
(ALL IN THE SAME WORLD)

BEASTLY TALES

Depravity

Deceit

Devastation

TALES OF CINDER

Disowned (prequel) *

Defiant

Disdain

Damnation

TALES OF SNOW

Despair

Desire

Degradation

RESURRECTION CHRONICLES
(hottie fey!)

Demon Ember	*Demon Night*	*Demon Fall*
Demon Flames	*Demon Dawn*	*Demon Kept **
Demon Ash	*Demon Disgrace*	*Demon Blind **
Demon Escape	*Demon Design **	*Demon Defeat - 1*
Demon Deception	*Demon Discord **	*Demon Defeat - 2*

* novella

A RESURRECTION CHRONICLES NOVELLA

DEMON SHOCK

M.J. HAAG

Shattered Glass
— PUBLISHING —

DEMON SHOCK. Copyright © 2025 by Melissa Haag. All rights reserved.
Published by Shattered Glass Publishing.
Print Cover design by Shattered Glass Publishing
© Depositphotos.com
Editing by The Proof Posse (Jackie, Dawn, Heather, Mirjam, and Roxanne)

ISBN 978-1-63869-063-4 (eBook Edition)
ISBN 978-1-63869-064-1 (Paperback Edition)

Version 2025.03.29

To Jackie
I'm grateful your life crossed paths with mine.
You will be missed.

CHAPTER ONE

AVA

I SAT BACK AND GRINNED AT MY COMPUTER SCREEN. MY REFLECTION didn't look the best. The circles under my blue eyes were noticeably dark, and I was overdue for a shower. But at least I couldn't see how greasy my long brown hair was with it thrown up in a sloppy swish.

Finally, after months of non-stop coding, the system conversion was complete and bug-free. I couldn't wait to see Steve's face. He'd said it wasn't possible within six months. For him, probably not. For me? I wasn't married, didn't have kids, and had no problem hiding away from the world to work non-stop for the fifty thousand dollar bonus the group had promised.

My laughter rang out in the silent cabin, startling my furry companions curled up on a nearby pillow.

"It's done. Finally. Aren't you excited?"

Pete and Repeat meowed at me when I stood with a stretch.

"This calls for a celebration, boys. What do you say? Should I head into town for some steak and lobster?"

Pete stood and strolled toward the kitchen. Repeat was right on his heels, and I chuckled.

"Ramen and tuna it is. I'm going to need to have my blood work done after this. It's probably fifty percent broth by now."

They made their small "mrr" sounds as if agreeing as I joined them and opened a can of tuna from the stack on the counter.

When I'd accepted the project, I'd prepped my grandparents' single-room cabin, stocking the root cellar's shelves below the cabin with canned and dried goods–stuff that was easy to prepare because I hadn't wanted to spend my time cooking. So obviously, tuna, spam, and ramen were in surplus, but other essentials were in surplus, too. And I had the propane tank out back topped off last October with enough fuel to run the backup generator when the sun was too weak for the solar panels to keep the lights and my computer on.

Other than the occasional outgoing email to update my manager on the project's status, I'd kept myself completely disconnected from the outside world, only leaving the cabin to use the bathroom.

The solitude hadn't only been productive; it'd been rejuvenating. Maybe I could use the success of this project as proof of the benefits of working remotely in the future. No office drama. No small city apartment. I could move back home and help my mom and sister with Pops. The chances of my boss agreeing were low, but it was still worth a try.

"Think of all the pets you'd get if I worked from home," I said to Pete and Repeat.

After dividing the tuna between their bowls, I put on my boots and coat and went outside. The layer of snow covering the ground wasn't as deep as it had been a few days ago, and the crisp air hinted at spring.

As I walked around to the back of the cabin, I tipped my head back and inhaled deeply. A long, thin line of smoke rose from the chimney, and I smiled to myself.

I loved the peace of being out here and wasn't looking forward to returning to the office after this. However, my boss promised me a long vacation to compensate for the overtime. So, once I trained everyone on the updates, I planned on leaving Pete and Repeat with Mom and Kylie and booking a two-week stay at an all-inclusive resort staffed by hot guys who enjoyed serving margaritas.

Would I even know what to do with a hot guy anymore? I grinned to myself and tried to remember how long it had been since my last date. A year? A year and a half? Too many failed attempts had left me averse to trying again. But the idea of someone to snuggle with late into the morning always pulled me back in eventually. Maybe a vacation fling would keep me safely out of the dating pool for a little longer.

Mentally picturing myself in a bikini, I opened the door to the external bathroom and stepped inside. I loved this oddity about the old cabin. It gave me a reason to go outside every day, even when I was working.

Situated next to the chimney, it was always toasty warm in winter. If it got too warm, I could prop the exterior door open and use the screen door, which was a must in the warmer months to keep the bugs out.

The tankless water heater worked like a charm, too. While showering, I tackled the reforestation occurring on my legs after a month of neglect and killed the razor. It was a worthy sacrifice, though. Without it, people in town would have thought Big Foot was real when they saw me get out of my truck—not that I was thinking about showing my legs until the temps reached above freezing.

I grabbed some clean clothes off the shelf and dressed, feeling like a newer, freer—and richer—person.

Back inside the cabin, I let my hair dry by the fire and contemplated calling or emailing my boss. If I called, I'd be opening Pandora's box. Everyone in the office would know I turned my phone back on and would inundate me with calls. If I emailed, I could let my boss know it was done and when I planned to return, then take a few well-earned days to myself.

Email it was.

I sat at my desk and wrote the most humble chest-beating

email I could manage, addressed to my boss and cc'd to Steve. With an unhealthy amount of vindication, I hit send.

Pete jumped up on my desk and went to sit on my keyboard. I quickly scooped him up to snuggle him.

"What do you think? Should we stay another week and then head back?"

He purred as I scratched between his ears. "Yeah, that's what I was thinking too."

My computer pinged with a new email, an unfamiliar sound since I usually turned off my internet connection after I hit send.

I released Pete. Repeat immediately jumped into my arms. Laughing, I shifted him to one side to check the reply. I hoped it was Steve with his same "it's not possible" speech so I could tell him to sit on a pole. However, it wasn't from him or my boss. It was an automated message saying it was undeliverable.

Actually, the last several email updates had all come back undeliverable. Looking at the dates, I started to drown in my panic. It'd been months since my boss had heard from me. Cringing, I started my phone and began troubleshooting my internet connection on my computer while I waited.

My phone and computer received errors that they couldn't connect to the server or carrier.

It wasn't the first time I had lost my satellite connection at the cabin. I was almost two hours northeast of Duluth, Minnesota, surrounded by towering trees. It happened.

Thankfully, I'd done all my programming on my local machines, so I hadn't lost any work—just maybe my job since I hadn't been providing the promised updates.

"I'll need to make a trip to town, no matter what, boys."

I put away anything they might knock over and banked the fire.

"No fighting," I said before shutting them in.

I parked my truck in the shed-turned-garage with the generator. The door rolled open with ease, and I patted the hood of my truck.

"Don't worry. We're not returning to civilization yet. Just to the highway to get a signal."

Navigating the dirt roads that led to the paved county road took longer than normal. At times, the roads were covered in a full winter's worth of virgin snow, making it difficult to tell where they were. So, I took it slow.

When I reached the paved road, I saw snow covering that, too, to my surprise. A lot of snow…as if it hadn't been plowed either. Only faint divots hinted at snowed-over tire marks. Since it was one of the main roads into Silver Bay, I found it kind of odd.

I checked my satellite phone for a signal but didn't find one. No surprise there. The overcast sky hinted at more snow, which wasn't uncommon in March this far north.

Turning onto the main road headed into town, I listened to the snow crunch under my tires.

The truck rumbled steadily for the first ten miles until I saw the curve that intersected with Lax Lake Road. I slowed down even more so I wouldn't end up in a ditch with no cell reception to call for a tow.

Snow covered the only house and driveway on the bend, untouched like the road. No smoke drifted from the chimney. They were probably already somewhere else enjoying beach-side margaritas, lucky bastards.

When I finally reached Silver Bay's subdivisions, I thought I'd see some road maintenance, but nope…the snow-covered pavement continued undisturbed. Maybe the city plow broke? But what about the sidewalks then? People usually cleared those.

A sense of wrongness crept down my spine as I noticed not a single person outside. Yes, it was cold. But people born in the upper Midwest didn't stay inside because of snow. It took extreme windchills to force them indoors. And the weather wasn't extreme. It was barely below freezing today.

I drove past the high school and saw the empty parking lot. Did I have the wrong day?

I glanced at my watch. It was a Tuesday in March. Spring break, maybe then?

Unable to shake the feeling that something was wrong, I pulled into the hardware store's parking lot and tried my satellite phone again. When I saw I still had no signal, I sighed and killed the engine.

The wind off the lake almost tore the door from my hand as I opened it. My boots crunched on the thin layer of wind-blown snow as I hurried toward the hardware store's door. I was busy keeping my head down to protect myself from the wind, so I didn't look up until I'd almost reached the door. When I did, my steps slowed.

The glass on the bottom half of the door was broken. Snow swept through the space, creating a drift just inside the door. I stared at the drift, or rather, the pant leg peeking out of the drift. Like a doomed moth drawn to the flame, I couldn't stop moving forward. I needed to know I was wrong. That my eyes were wrong.

A step closer, the rest of the man came into view. He lay slouched against a display case. Frozen solid with a bullet hole between his lifeless, half-closed eyes.

My breathing came in sharp rasps as I peddled back rapidly and fell on my ass. I sprang right back up and bolted to my truck.

I had no phone, and there was nobody around to flag down. Why weren't there people around? Someone should have found him already. He'd looked like he'd been there for days.

My hands shook as I started the engine and turned my truck around.

With a growing sense of panic, I scanned the unmarred parking lot of the police station right across the street. Where was everyone?

Spinning out of the parking lot, I drove into the closest subdivision, peering at the houses. I spotted a broken window and a front door ajar. A few yards had snow-covered lumps on them.

I wiped a shaking hand across my face, unsure when I'd started crying, and turned onto the main road to check another subdivision. All the houses were the same. Devoid of any signs of life. The same with the next and the next. I snaked my way through every street in Silver Bay then stopped in the middle of the road.

A whole town…empty. How? Why?

I glanced at the house on my right, debating whether to go inside. Nothing looked off about it, yet I feared what I'd find.

With a pitiful groan of defeat, I turned into the driveway and parked the truck. The silence when I got out this time was more noticeable without the wind. The crunch of snow under my boots seemed louder.

I knocked on the door and waited for an answer—a whisper of noise, anything to indicate someone was there. Hearing nothing, I tried the knob. It turned freely, and the door opened with a crackle of ice breaking free around the jamb. Proof it'd been a long while since it'd been opened.

My breath fogged inside as I called out a tentative hello. Lit by the overcast dimness from outside, the words spray painted on the wall had an extra level of eeriness.

We waited as long as we could. We're sorry. Go to Phil's. We won't evacuate without you. Be safe. Don't trust anyone. See you soon. Love, Mom and Dad.

I stared at the words. Evacuate?

My thoughts drifted back over the last few months. While at the cabin, I hadn't seen or heard anything. Not buried in the woods like I'd been.

Pivoting on my heel, I returned to my truck and started home with one question ringing in my mind: *What in the hell had happened?*

CHAPTER TWO

GYRIK

"How does it look?" Will asked.

Crouched low, I studied the group waiting at the snow-covered crossroads below. After days of broadcasting on the shortwave radio, a man had finally responded that his group was running low on supplies.

Since humans didn't trust one another—too many would hurt their own kind for supplies, no matter how meager—we'd arrived at the meetup place he'd designated early enough to observe the group for a time.

"One near the car is moving like he's anxious. The others are calmer. I don't see any weapons." I paused as a car door opened, and a person wearing a dress emerged.

"What?" Will asked. "You just did that blink thing you do when you're confused."

"I..." I didn't know what to say. My brothers and I had lived thousands of years without understanding what a female was because we'd had none of our own. However, since coming to the surface and discovering human females, we saw and appreciated their uniqueness. Each one had their own version of beauty. But the one warming her hands below was...

"We're leaving in two seconds if you don't say something," Will said.

"Do males wear women's clothing?" I asked, finally tearing my gaze from the group to look at Will.

We'd been together for weeks, searching the northern Midwest for survivors. So I was used to Will and how he grinned at me when he found my lack of knowledge entertaining. It didn't bother me. I knew I still had much to learn.

He grinned at me now. "Some men did before the world went to shit. Not sure how many still would now. The world outside of our sanctuaries seems even meaner than it was. Why are you asking?"

"I think a male is wearing a dress to pretend he is female. He looks pretty, but...not?"

Will laughed and clapped my back.

"This sounds like another trap. Let's head down and see if they'll trade information for food. No getting shot, okay?"

We crept backward until we could stand without being noticed by the group below, and I stayed near the trees while Will jogged back toward the vehicles parked along the side of the snow-covered road.

He grabbed the radio as he closed his door, and I listened to him tell Zach and Bram to stay where they were. Bram gave me a thumbs-up from his vehicle as Will started the engine and left to head toward the meetup site.

Watching the group in the valley below, I tried not to feel the disappointment and hopelessness that wanted to consume me. We'd been looking for survivors for weeks, and although we'd made contact with several groups like the one today, we hadn't found a single female.

Were the only surviving females in Tolerance and Tenacity? I hoped not. I'd already spoken to those females more than once, and none of them had any interest in me.

I rubbed the ache in my chest and reminded myself of the maps Bram had shown me. The North American continent was vast. It would take us years to search it and even more to explore the other continents.

Patience, I reminded myself. *You will find the perfect female eventually.*

When I knew Will was getting close, I waved to Zach and Bram and ran down the hill.

I reached the trees alongside the group as Will's vehicle approached.

"Get ready," the one wearing the dress said in a deep voice. "Don't shoot until we know where the supplies are."

I sighed at hearing the confirmation that they had weapons. Too many humans were like that now. Angry. Demanding. More concerned about taking than contributing.

Will cut the engine and threw the keys on the dash. Then he got out of the vehicle and raised his hands up, palms out.

He insisted we give each group a chance to prove their worth. I understood why—there were so few humans left—but I also hated that Will, a good man, risked his life to test the worthiness of others.

"My name's Will," he said. "Who did I speak with on the radio?"

"Me," a man said. "Adree. What did you bring?"

Will smiled. "Help if you want it. We have a community farther south. Greenhouses. Self-sufficiency. Cows. Chickens. Hell, they even found some goats. Not sure what we'll do with those yet, but they're pretty entertaining to watch."

A few of the men exchanged glances.

"So you didn't bring supplies," Adree said.

"We've found that traveling with handouts only gets us robbed," Will said.

One man swore and reached behind him for the weapon he hid there.

In a blur, I sprinted into their midst, disarming and knocking them out with a light tap to their heads until only the person in the dress remained standing. Although I'd taken his weapon, I hesitated to make him sleep like the others. Mom said that women could grow facial hair, but she'd said it usually was very light. My gaze dipped to his-her chest. Not all females had discernible breasts.

"You're going to need to get undressed," Will said, standing beside me as I stared at the person.

"Why?"

"Because you're confusing him," Will said. "He needs to know if you're actually a woman."

He-she glanced at me. I could see the revulsion and fear but also the anger and hate. Emotions I often saw when both males and females looked at me.

"What the fuck is he?" the person asked.

"He's one of the guys who helped kill most of the infected a few weeks ago. Might want to be nice and listen."

The man stripped, and I knocked him unconscious once I saw his penis.

"Sorry he wasn't a she," Will said, clapping me on the shoulder. "Maybe this group has a bigger home base like we do. But even if these guys don't have some single ladies tucked away somewhere, I'm sure we'll find one eventually."

He moved off and started tying up the unconscious men. I lifted the naked one and tugged his dress over his head before tying his hands and tossing him back into the vehicle so he wouldn't get cold.

When I faced Will, he had one man propped up and was tapping his face as our second vehicle came rumbling along the road.

"Time to wake up, sunshine," Will said.

When the man didn't respond, Will reached into his pocket for one of the vials that smelled so bad it woke unconscious humans. The man coughed as he came to.

"There you are," Will said.

The man's dazed gaze drifted to me. His eyes went wide, and he screamed at the same time he tried to climb over Will to get away from me. Will slapped him hard. He claimed it was the best way to shake a person out of their shock. I didn't think it left a better impression of me.

With my grey skin, pointed ears, and yellow-green eyes, I'd not yet seen a human welcome one of my kind the first time they saw us. My extra height and bulk didn't make me any less intimidating to new people.

The man froze and stared at Will as he gasped for breath.

"You have a choice to make here," Will said. "You can tell us about your base and receive a week's worth of rations, or you can say nothing, and we'll find your base on our own, and you get nothing."

The man's fear-filled gaze flicked to me again. Then to Bram and Zach, who joined us.

"Wha-wha-what is he?" the man stuttered.

Zach grinned at me. This part of meeting new people amused him. He said it was better to be the one scaring people than to be the one scared.

"He's our friend," Will said. "And we're interested in making more friends, not enemies. You understand me?"

The man nodded.

"After pulling guns on me when I was clearly unarmed, we're not off to a good start."

"Wh-what do you want to know?" the man asked, his gaze shifting between me, Will, and Bram and Zach. "I'll tell you anything."

"How many of you are back at your camp or base, or whatever you call it? Are there any women or children? Are they being mistreated or kept against their will?"

How many times had I heard Will ask these questions now? Six? Seven times? The ache in my chest returned, but I didn't rub it now. I focused on the frightened male watching me.

"Everyone you see here and three more back at the homestead," he said. "Adree's grandma is still with us. She's not doing well, but she's not mistreated. It's why we need the supplies."

Grandma was a term humans used to address aged females like Mary. I liked Mary. She was kind and washed my clothes for me and liked to pat my thigh. It saddened me that another grandma like Mary wasn't doing well.

"What's wrong with her?" Will asked.

"Age. She was forgetting things before this all started. She's been getting weaker, too. Doesn't like to get out of bed. Adree takes care of her."

"What does she need?" Will asked.

"Just more food. She doesn't eat much, even when Adree mashes it up for her."

"Any chance you're lying to us?"

The male's gaze flicked to me again. "I'd be stupid to do that at this point, don't you think?"

Will untied the man's hands and stepped back so Bram could hand him a box of spare rations. "If it gets too hard out here or if you just need help, head south toward Warrensburg. It's a place East of Kansas City. Avoid the city. The bombs hit it hard, but infected still wander around in there."

The man nodded, and we left him to wake his people while we followed their tracks back to their place in our vehicles.

I climbed a tree and watched the house for a while. Two people moved around, just as the man had said. I didn't see or hear any sign of women or children.

Will was waiting for me at the base of the tree when I jumped down.

"What do you think?" he asked.

"I think he was telling the truth. I didn't see any signs of women or children, and the house has been secured against infected."

"Okay. Then we'll mark the map. Any idea where you want to head next?"

I looked around at the trees and found my gaze drifting to the north.

"We should continue north."

He nodded, and Bram took a map of the state from the truck and spread it out on the hood.

"This is where we are. Where's your gut telling us we should go next?" Bram asked.

Over the last few weeks, we'd worked our way steadily from Tolerance just listening to my instincts, which they trusted. Although mine weren't as good as Molev's, our leader, they'd kept us from serious trouble so far. And because of them, we'd found several groups of people along the way. But no females. I was starting to doubt myself even as my gaze was drawn to another area on the map.

"Here," I said, pointing to a town along the lake Will called "Superior," even though it wasn't the largest lake on the maps I'd seen.

"We should make it there before dark," Will said. "Hopefully, we'll find a place with the heat still on."

"And a freezer full of steaks," Zach said, hopeful anticipation adding an extra bounce to his step.

Unfortunately, we didn't find either of those things in Silver Bay. However, we did find fresh tire tracks in the snow.

"What do you think?" Will asked as he rolled to a stop. "People looking for supplies or trouble?"

"They didn't stop," I said. "No footprints are leading away from the marks."

"What does that mean?"

"If they wanted supplies, they would have stopped and checked the houses. I think they were looking for something else."

I searched for any sign of what they might have wanted.

One of the snow piles in the yard closest to us moved then settled.

"Stay here," I said.

I left the vehicle and jogged to the mound. The infected under the snow was still alive, but its clothes had frozen to the ground. I removed its head so that, once the weather warmed and it thawed, it wouldn't be a danger to anyone.

Will turned off the engine and got out. "We might as well do a full sweep before we follow those tracks back to whoever left them."

I looked up at the darkening sky.

"We need to hurry. It'll snow soon."

CHAPTER THREE

AVA

It took two hours and a lot of cat snuggles for my hands to stop shaking. And another two hours to figure out what I should do. I'd never hated being single more in my entire life. Screw serenity. I wanted someone to tell me everything was okay and not as fucked up as it had looked.

I set another bag by the door and went to my computer. It was the last thing I needed to pack before I buried myself under a pile of blankets and crashed.

The stress of the day and my whirlwind thoughts were catching up with me. I just wanted to forget everything and finish packing so I could head out at first light.

However, scenes from earlier kept replaying in my head. The undisturbed, snow-covered roads as I'd left. The quiet town. The broken door. The dead man. But what I kept coming back to was the writing on the wall.

Evacuations. Don't trust anyone.

What did it all mean? What had happened? *When* had it happened?

The only way to figure any of that out was to leave the cabin and head somewhere that might have news. Silver Bay had been the closest town. Duluth was the nearest big city. After that, the twin cities.

While I knew I could drive to Duluth and back in a day, I wasn't sure what I'd find. What if Duluth was empty like Silver Bay? Even as I told myself that wasn't possible, part of me feared it might be.

Don't trust anyone.

"Is there anyone even left to trust?" I asked Pete.

He did his little questioning "mrr" back at me.

"I know I only checked Silver Bay, but you didn't see what I saw, Pete. There weren't any tracks on the roads, and that guy… he'd been like that for a while. Someone would've found him if there were more people around. And the evacuation message on the wall really makes me think there aren't.

"If Silver Bay was evacuated, a clean-up crew should have come in to help fix whatever caused the evacuation. The only disaster I saw was the missing people. It wasn't like there was ten feet of snow or a blizzard or anything. It's just a normal Minnesota winter out there. That means it wasn't a natural disaster, Pete. And if it wasn't that, then what was it? How far out does it go? Duluth? The cities? I hope Kylie is with Mom and Pops."

Pete started purring, which helped me feel a little calmer as I packed away the cords. Once I was done, I left the box on the desk, stoked the fire, and checked the time.

It was just after nine.

"One last bathroom run, guys," I said. "Keep the bed warm for me."

I bundled up and let myself out of the cabin. A heavy, wet snow had started falling about an hour ago. If not for the light from the side window, the way around the cabin would have been pitch black. It didn't matter though. I'd been here so long that I could walk the path to the bathroom with my eyes closed.

The crunch of wet snow under my boots muffled the sound of my light breathing. I didn't fully notice either noise. My thoughts were still whirling with what I'd need to do when I woke up and the problems I might encounter along the way. Did the truck have enough gas? What if I got stuck?

Preoccupied, I turned the corner of the cabin and almost ran into the man standing there.

A startled "eep" ripped from me, and I vaguely saw him raise his hands above his head in an "I surrender" pose as I backpedaled and pressed a hand to my thundering heart.

"I won't hurt you," he said quickly, hands still above his head.

It took a few seconds to understand the significance of the moment.

I wasn't alone.

Relief and gratitude flooded me. With another cry, I threw myself into his torso and wrapped my arms around his waist. He was big. Solid. The tears from fear I hadn't even realized I'd been keeping at bay poured out of me in wracking sobs.

"It's okay," he said. "You're okay."

One of his large hands lightly settled on the top of my head. It felt so good. So comforting.

"I'm sorry I scared you."

He thought I was crying because of him? I shook my head against his chest.

"I went to Silver Bay," I said through my tears. "There was a dead guy in the hardware store, and no one else was there."

I sniffled and wiped my face on my coat sleeve without releasing him.

"I thought I was alone."

"Isn't there anyone else here?"

The question rang like a gong in my head, and in my mind, I saw the words on the wall.

Don't trust anyone.

My tears instantly dried up as my pulse kicked up a notch. I'd been so relieved I wasn't alone that common sense had vanished. What sane woman hugged a strange man in the dark? Alone?

18

None. Although, after the day I'd had, could I still claim to be sane?

I released my hold on him and would have backed up, but he wrapped an arm around my shoulders to keep me pinned against his chest. My cheek brushed his tear-dampened shirt.

"Please let me go," I said, trying to keep my voice steady.

"Will you run?"

I was thinking about it, but I sure as hell wasn't going to tell him that.

"No."

He slowly released me, and I stepped back to look up at him. The light from the cabin was too dim to see him clearly, but I saw his general shape. He towered over me by a good foot and a half. The large, solid stature I'd found comforting only moments ago now seemed more threatening. I wished I could see his face to read his expression.

I waited for him to say something, but he didn't.

"Do you know what happened in Silver Bay?" I asked finally.

"I think most of the people evacuated," he said.

"A house I checked had a message about evacuation. From what?"

"The infected."

His answer confused and worried me. "People were sick? How long ago? Will I get sick?"

I hadn't touched the dead man, but I'd been close enough to him. I'd also gone into that house.

"It was months ago. You won't get sick unless you're bitten."

Bitten? Was he serious?

"Were you bitten?" he asked.

"No. Is that why you wanted to know if there's anyone else here? Are you afraid we're sick?"

"No. I heard you talking to Pete."

"Oh." I wasn't sure I wanted to tell him Pete was my cat, even though I'd pretty much already confessed I was alone.

The silence between us stretched until I shifted from one foot to the other. Why was he here? What did he want? If the sickness was months ago, why was that guy still in the hardware store?

"Are you cold?" he asked.

"No. I'm okay. Where did you come from?"

"Missouri. My brothers and I helped survivors build a community safe from the infected and the hounds."

Missouri? That was a haul from here. And survivors? That didn't sound good. It couldn't be that bad. And… "Hounds?"

"How long have you been here?" he asked.

"Since the beginning of November. About five months now."

"And you heard nothing? No howls? No bombing?"

"Bombing?" He was freaking me out now. No…*he* wasn't. What he was saying was. He seemed pretty calm, which was good. I needed a lot of calm.

I saw him reach up to run his hand over his head and saw that he didn't have a hat. Neither did I. I reached up and felt how wet my hair was getting.

While I didn't want to invite him inside, I also didn't want him to leave. He obviously knew more than I did. Was he safe, though?

Don't trust anyone.

Did I have any choice? He was the first person I'd seen alive in months. Would I be stupid to send him away and head out on my own in the morning without a clue about what was going on? Yes, I would be.

"Listen, I have a lot of questions that I think you can answer. If I invite you inside, what are the chances I'm going to end up hurt or used in some way?"

"There will be no chances. I won't let anything hurt you. I promise."

He'd said "anything," not "anyone," which I found weird and concerning. But I didn't see that I had any other option if I wanted answers.

"Okay. Then, if you don't mind waiting another minute, I'm going to use the bathroom that's behind you first."

He stepped aside, and I moved to grab the screen door handle.

"My name's Ava, by the way."

"My name is Gyrik."

Gear-ick. A unique name. I kind of liked it.

"It's nice to meet you, Gyrik. And I hope that doesn't change in the near future."

I closed myself in the bathroom, turned on the light, and glanced at the door, wishing it had a lock. Since it didn't, I hurried to use the toilet, washed my hands and face, and brushed my teeth for the night. Once I was finished, I hesitated to open the door.

"Are you still out there, Gyrik?"

"Yes."

"I'm curious. If you're from Missouri, why are you all the way up here?"

"We're looking for survivors. There aren't many humans left."

I turned my head to look at myself in the mirror. My "I'm in so much trouble" expression was for two reasons.

One...he'd just said what I'd feared. That there weren't many of us left.

Two...humans? Why did he say that like he wasn't one?

"Because of the sickness?" I asked.

"Yes."

"Are you sick?"

"No. My brothers and I are immune. That's why we were able to save so many humans. Most humans scream when they first see us or hate us because we look different. Thank you for not screaming and for hugging me instead. It's the first time I've been welcomed like that."

Humans? He and his brothers looked different? Part of me wondered if I'd just hugged some kind of crazy person who would murder me in my sleep. But not everything he was saying sounded crazy.

If I hadn't spent hours driving around Silver Bay, I would have thought all the talk about sickness was a setup for some kind of practical joke.

But I knew it wasn't. There hadn't been a soul in Silver Bay.

I stared at the door, really, really not wanting to open it. But damn if I wasn't curious too.

"Are you all right?" he asked.

"Not really," I admitted. "I've been alone for months, and it didn't bother me at all. But if you're telling the truth, which there's a good chance you are, I've been more alone than I realized, and it's kind of terrifying."

"You don't need to be afraid. You're not alone anymore. I'm here. I promise I won't leave you. And, if you want, I can take you back to Missouri. There are people like you there."

"People who didn't know the world ended?"

"No, people who survived it."

I'd survived something without even knowing it. How? Why?

"Are you going to come out, Ava? It's snowing harder now."

After taking a steadying breath, I opened the door. The light from the bathroom illuminated the immediate area and the man standing in it.

He was huge, both in height and muscle. He wore leather pants that molded to his legs, leather boots that reached mid-calf, and a dark T-shirt. Everything about him blended with the shadows behind him, even his grey skin.

Grey.

My gaze swept up to his face, and I froze.

"Most humans scream when they first see us or hate us because we look different. Thank you for not screaming."

Don't you dare scream, Ava, I told myself as I stared at his very non-human eyes.

A golden outer ring surrounded his yellow-green irises and vertical pupil. Vertical like a cat's. His ears were pointed, too, and clearly visible, thanks to his close-cropped hair.

It all looked real. How?

The tip of his ear grew darker as I stared, and he reached up to rub his ear. The gesture screamed nervousness.

I was making *him* nervous?

"I think I missed a lot while I was here," I said faintly.

He nodded slowly. "I think so, too."

"Would you like to come inside the cabin? I'd really like to hear about what happened."

Without waiting for his reply, I turned off the bathroom light and closed the door behind me.

The chaos in my brain whispered that he might kill me before I reached the front. But it also said I'd probably die of some mysterious sickness anyway, so I didn't see how my fear even mattered.

CHAPTER FOUR

GYRIK

I'D FINALLY DONE IT. AFTER WEEKS OF SEARCHING FOR MORE survivors, I'd found a female.

Ava.

She was the prettiest female I'd ever seen. Her soft, straight brown hair reached the middle of her back and smelled sweet, like her skin. I watched it sway as she turned away from me.

My gaze swept over her length. Most females had to look up at us. Ava was no different. The top of her head had reached my collarbone when she'd hugged me. I could still feel the way her cheek had pressed against my chest, right over my heart. Had she heard how hard it had beat from her sudden embrace?

I couldn't believe how she'd welcomed me. She hadn't been angry or eager to leave. She actually wanted to talk to me even more, and I was glad. I liked the sound of her voice. It was low and soft.

When she'd looked up at me, her eyes had reminded me of the sky heavy with storm clouds, blue and grey. Her gaze hadn't held any hate. Only a little fear. And I didn't think it was because of me. She didn't seem to know what had happened to her world.

Would it be smarter to call Bram, Will, and Zach to talk to her? I listened to how her heart raced and watched her tuck her trembling hands into her pockets as we retraced her steps around the cabin in the dark. I knew she would probably feel more comfortable with her own kind. Yet, I hesitated to get them.

She'd hugged *me*.

The feel of her arms around my waist lingered. I didn't want her to hug the others. Perhaps she would hold me again if I was the only one there. I really wanted that. She was the first female ever to hug me.

When she reached the door, she paused and looked back at me. Her gaze held mine then flicked to my ears briefly before sweeping over me from my head to my feet.

Her study made me nervous. Would she grow to hate me like the others? I tried to remember everything I'd learned about women.

Don't look at her breasts.

Don't tell her she's pretty first. Tell her she's smart.

Don't ask to see her pussy.

Don't say the word pussy.

Don't think of her pussy.

Because I was thinking of her pussy, I wanted to look down even though she was clothed and I knew I wouldn't see anything.

My pulse raced again, and I fought to keep my gaze on hers.

Don't show her you're desperate.

I knew so many rules for what *not* to do but nothing about what *to* do when a female looked at me expectantly. I tried to think of something to say, but she turned away and went inside before I could.

She didn't close the door, though.

She's welcoming me.

Trying not to move too quickly, I followed her in. Her sweet scent teased my nose, and I found myself leaning toward her a little to breathe it in again. She moved away and shut the door, closing us into her home together.

The inside was warm and small. It reminded me of my home

in Ernisi but softer. A chair waited near the fire, and her bed wasn't far from that.

She sat on the chair and gestured for me to sit on the bed.

I saw two cats sleeping peacefully near her pillow. We had one in Tolerance. It was soft, but it didn't like to be disturbed. So I cautiously lowered my weight at the end of the bed, away from the cats.

Ava watched me and glanced at the cats.

"Are you allergic to cats?" she asked.

"No. I didn't want to wake them."

She smiled slightly. It wasn't full of humor, though. I saw her exhaustion and fear and wanted to comfort her, but I wasn't sure how.

"Will you tell me what happened?" she asked.

"It is a long story, and you look tired. Would you like to sleep first?"

"No, I don't think I'll be able to sleep for a while."

I nodded and started from the beginning I knew. I explained how my brothers and I had lived underground for thousands of years, not knowing other people existed on the surface or that there even was a surface until an earthquake made an opening.

Ava listened to my explanation of the hounds that had escaped from my world. How they'd bitten her people and had started the spread of an infection.

"We didn't know anything about humans. When the first of my brothers came to the surface, they killed many humans by removing their heads. They did not know that meant death here. In our caves, we would be reborn. Mya, the first human female one of my brothers discovered, helped him understand. We don't kill humans anymore, not even the bad ones who hurt other humans."

Ava looked down at her hands and let out a long breath. After a long silence, she asked, "Are there a lot of bad ones?"

"Yes. But there are many good ones, too."

She laughed humorlessly and wiped her hands on her loose

grey pants. "Not much has changed in that regard then. So that's what happened to all the people? They got sick and died?"

"No. They became infected and tried to infect others. Your people evacuated the healthy people from the big cities and bombed the infected that remained."

"Cities were bombed?"

I nodded. "Many. Initially, the infected were stupid, so they didn't run away. They ran toward the sound."

"Biting...stupid...the way you're describing them sounds like they were zombies or something."

"That's what Zach called them. Zombies. Undead."

Ava's already pale complexion grew paler.

I began to doubt the wisdom of telling her everything. I remembered how frightened the infected made humans. If Ava hadn't ever seen one yet, perhaps—

"Okay." She nodded. "Zombies. What happened next?"

I hesitated but caved under the weight of her expectant gaze.

"They were stupid and easy to kill in the beginning. But after a few weeks, they got smarter. They started working with the hounds. They wanted to kill all the humans that were left. Andie, another female who survived, brought scientists who helped us discover how the infected and hounds were linked. Once we destroyed the link, the hounds and the smart infected died. Now, only the stupid infected are left.

"They're still very dangerous. You shouldn't let one bite you."

"Yeah, that sounds like a smart idea." A pinkish hue slowly tinted her cheeks. "So, you and your brothers live with other human survivors in Missouri? And it's safe there? None of those infected are around?"

"Some are still drawn to us by sound, but the community has high walls, so the infected can't get in."

She wiped her hands on her pants again.

"Are you too warm? Would you like to take off your coat?" I asked.

"I don't think I'm ready to do that yet."

I didn't understand why. Her cheeks were growing redder, and she was sitting next to the fire. I knew humans preferred their living spaces warmer, but Ava's home was even warmer than Mary and James' house, which they kept warmer than the others because they were older.

Perhaps Ava had a human sickness called a cold.

"Would you like to lie down?" I asked.

She shook her head. "Why are you looking for survivors?"

I considered how to answer. Angel's warning not to sound desperate rang in my head.

"You said that you and your brothers came to the surface and that your brother, Drav, discovered Mya, a woman. Are you collecting women?"

My mind went blank. I knew I couldn't admit we were looking for women and children. Eden said that made us sound like men who only wanted sex. I did want to have sex, though. Eventually. Hopefully with Ava. I wanted to inhale her scent again and feel her arms around me.

"You just blinked like you're trying to send Morse code," Ava said.

"I don't want to say anything that will scare you."

"Too late for that, I think. You just told me I'm living in the aftermath of a worldwide zombie apocalypse. I'd rather know the truth about what's going on. Are you collecting women?"

Rather than answering the direct question, I told her my group's purpose.

"I'm with three other humans. We're looking for survivors. Males and females. We've found a few groups. Most of them were males. The good ones, who didn't try to hurt us or take our supplies, we offered to let them join us. They chose not to. We marked the bad ones on a map so we can come back and check on them later. Will says it's a way to police them and ensure they won't hurt others."

"So you're offering anyone who's nice a place in your community?"

"Yes."

"What about me? Do you consider me nice?"

My cock twitched at how nice I considered her.

"Yes."

"You gave me a lot to think about. How soon do you need an answer?"

Hope lit inside of me.

"How long would you like to think about it?"

"Can you give me until the morning?"

I nodded and stood, eager to return to the others and share the news with them. When I stood, so did she. She walked me to the door and didn't close it as soon as I was outside.

Pausing, I turned back to look at her.

"Thank you for welcoming me into your home. I will see you in the morning."

"See you in the morning, Gyrik."

She closed the door, and I smiled wide enough that my teeth reflected in the window beside the door. She'd hugged me, talked to me without screaming, and remembered my name.

Turning on my heel, I sprinted away from the cabin.

Our campsite was several miles away, down an unused dirt road near hers. Will had the fire going and a tent set up. The entrance was open, and I could see Will and Zach in their sleeping bags inside. They didn't like to sleep with the entrance closed when I wasn't there. They said they felt more comfortable being able to see and hear what was happening.

I jumped over the wire Will had strung around the camp and landed several feet away from Bram, which made him jump.

"Sorry," I said quickly. "I found a female."

"Seriously?" Zach asked, sitting up in his sleeping bag.

"Yes. Her name is Ava. She has pretty blue eyes and a soft voice like her body. She didn't scream when she saw me and invited me into her house."

"Was it made out of gingerbread?" Zach asked with a grin.

"What is gingerbread?"

"Stop giving him a hard time," Bram said. "How big of a group is she with?"

"She's the only one. I watched and listened a long time before I approached. She'd been talking to Pete and Repeat, so I thought there were two males with her, but they are her cats."

"Seriously? She's alone out here with two cats?" Will said.

"And she didn't know anything happened," I said. "That's why she drove around Silver Bay. She was looking for people. She has her things packed like she was going to leave. It's good we found her."

Zach chuckled. "I bet she's like Eden and was just playing it cool around you until you left so she can run."

My stomach tightened at the thought, and I glanced at Bram for confirmation. He patted my shoulder consolingly.

"He might be right."

I glanced back in the direction of her cabin, feeling a thread of panic. I'd just found her. What if I lost her?

"Go keep an eye on her," Zach said. "But remember not to act like a stalker. Girls don't like that."

"Stalker?"

"Someone who forces their attention on someone else when it's not wanted," Bram said. "Don't overthink it. Just go keep her safe until first light. We'll join you then."

CHAPTER FIVE

AVA

I COULDN'T SLEEP. PETE WAS ACTING LIKE A PROTECTIVE HAT, purring contentedly on my pillow. Repeat was by my waist under the covers. We were in our cozy sleep pose, but I couldn't turn off my thoughts.

Everything Gyrik had said kept running through my head. Had I really worked my way through the zombie apocalypse? Was the entire world gone? Just like that?

The worst part was that my brain was stuck on the fact I'd wasted five months on something I would never get paid for. How dumb was that? I had no idea where my family was. If they were safe. How many people had died? What the hell Gyrik even was because, by his own admission, he wasn't human. Or the fact that he hadn't directly answered my question about whether they were collecting women.

All my mind wanted to obsess over was that dumb bonus— maybe because it was the easiest thing to process in the face of everything else.

With a sigh, I closed my eyes and tried to let it all go.

It must have worked because I woke up to daylight streaming through my windows and a knock at my door.

Groggy and out of sorts, I fumbled my way out of bed and opened the door without even asking who was there.

The sight of a tall black man caught me off guard. "Uh, can I help you?"

He smiled and chuckled.

"My name's Bram. Are you hungry? We have some beans and spam if you are."

It was the weirdest offer I'd ever gotten from a stranger who'd knocked on my door.

But then my brain kick-started, and current events resurfaced. I looked beyond Bram to see who "we" was. Another man and a teen were with Bram, and Gyrik was standing quite a few yards behind them.

He looked a lot different in the light of day. Bigger. Maybe a little scarier–but also not because of the way he nervously shifted his weight from one leg to the other as he rubbed a hand over the top of his short hair.

"You're Gyrik's friends?" I asked. "The ones looking for survivors."

"We are," Bram said. Then he pointed to his companions. "That's Will and Zach, and you've already met Gyrik."

Four men. One woman. I wasn't stupid. I was well aware of the inherent danger. Yet, heading to Duluth by myself to discover the truth of the story Gyrik had told me was more terrifying than the group at my door.

"Come in."

I stepped back so they could enter the cabin. Gyrik was slower than the rest, hesitating to approach as if I were the one to be afraid of. I waited patiently until he was inside then closed the door on the cold temperature outside.

"The past twenty-four hours have been really weird for me. I'm struggling to believe everything Gyrik said." I glanced at Gyrik. "Obviously, *something* happened."

"It's like he said," Zach said. "Earthquakes opened up these caverns where he and his brothers were living, releasing these cursed hellhounds that started attacking people. The hellhounds essentially started a zombie apocalypse. But don't worry. We're past the worst of it. Promise."

I laughed faintly because his cliff-noted version sounded as insane as Gyrik's more detailed version. Yet, Gyrik's appearance and what I'd seen in Silver Bay were proof enough to convince me it wasn't some crazy story.

"How many people got sick?" I asked.

Will and Bram exchanged a long look before Will said, "There aren't many of us left."

Exactly what Gyrik had said the night before. Had I hoped the answer would change? Absolutely.

"Okay then, what now? You're looking for people like me. You found one. What happens next?"

"Next, if you'd like, you can travel with us back to the community Gyrik told you about," Will said.

"And if I don't like?"

"You do what you want. We mark our map to indicate where we last saw you, and we check on you occasionally to make sure you're doing all right and offer help when we can."

That sounded reasonable and assuring.

In the back of my mind, I'd been worried it was some kind of enslavement thing. It still could be. They might be great liars. But why bother lying to me? There were four of them and one of me. If they wanted to do something, they could, and there wouldn't be much I could do to stop them.

"What are the chances I'm going to end up raped if I leave with the four of you?"

The three humans quickly held up their hands and retreated a step while voicing various denials.

Gyrik didn't move. He remained frozen in place as he stared at me with an odd expression. He looked lost and a little afraid.

If these men were acting, they were good at it. But I didn't think their reactions were an act any more than Silver Bay had been.

"I'm not accusing. Just checking," I said. "I didn't hear any vehicles, but I'm assuming you drove here, right?"

They nodded.

"Okay. Well, I have a truck I can have loaded within an hour to follow you. How long will it take to get to your place, and do you think I'll ever be able to come back here?"

They all looked fairly surprised that I'd agreed so quickly. I didn't know what other types of people they'd already come across, but I wasn't some survivalist, and I didn't want to face an unknown world alone.

Bram was the first to recover.

"It'll take us a few days. We'll be checking on people on the way back," he said. "And although it'll be possible to return here, I wouldn't count on it being easy forever. The fuel will eventually run out.

"We've been siphoning and scavenging abandoned vehicles along the way, which is probably what will happen to this place once you leave it. People come through, see it's empty, and check for supplies. So if you really want something, you should take it with you."

I nodded and looked around. There wasn't much in the way of sentimental items, just the cabin itself.

"We can help you load what you've packed," Zach said, gesturing to the stuff by the door.

"Thanks. There's stuff in the cellar, too, that I should take."

After months of just me, Pete, and Repeat, it felt weird to have so many people moving around the cabin. My cats didn't mind. They liked people and strolled up to whoever they fancied for pets and scratches, including Gyrik. Every time they would team up and wind between that giant man's legs to demand attention, he would freeze and then slowly crouch down to pet them.

Zach caught me watching him on one of his trips out.

"There aren't many pets where we're at."

"Will it be a problem if I bring them with me?"

"No," Gyrik said before Zach could answer. "They're not

problems." Repeat jumped up into his arms. Gyrik immediately started scratching the top of Repeat's head just the way he liked.

Zach chuckled, picked up the next box of canned goods, and walked out the door.

"They'll want you to hold them the whole way if you keep that up," I said.

Gyrik glanced up at me. "Can I hold them?"

"It's fine with me," I said with a shrug. "They'll let you know when they don't want to be held anymore."

Talking to him was getting easier. Looking at him, too. Every now and again, though, I would catch him watching me with his very cat-like gaze—the one that cats had right before they pounced—and I'd feel a little nervous. Will, Bram, and Zach didn't seem bothered by Gyrik's occasional intensity, though. So I tried not to be either.

"I think that's everything," Bram said, coming inside.

Since I'd changed and gotten ready when they'd started moving things out to the truck, there wasn't anything else for me to do but turn off the power and drain the lines for winterization. They watched me while I worked, and Will followed me into the shed where the generator and the battery bank were.

"Those batteries are a hot commodity," he said from behind me. "You should take them with you."

I nodded since I knew I probably wouldn't be coming back.

He made quick work of disconnecting the batteries and the generator. I didn't know what he planned to do with the big, heavy thing until he looked at Gyrik, who'd swapped Repeat for Pete.

"You're up, Gyrik," Will said.

Gyrik handed Pete to Bram, picked up the generator like it weighed nothing, and set it in the back of the utility truck they were driving. The bed barely moved.

"I don't think your truck would have handled the load," Bram said. "If you want to drive that one—"

"Nope, this is fine. I'm not worried about having something

taken away from me. I'm more worried about what I'm going to see once we leave."

Bram nodded sympathetically.

"It's not pretty, and the first infected you see will probably scare the…daylights out of you, but you've made it this far. You'll be fine. Just stick with Gyrik. He'll keep us safe."

Looking from the three men to Gyrik, who was reclaiming Pete, I decided that sticking to the giant who had an affinity for cats wouldn't be too difficult.

"Gyrik will ride with you if that's okay. He can keep an eye on things behind us, and I'll watch ahead." Bram handed Gyrik a handheld radio. "I'll let you know if I see anything that needs clearing."

Anxiety soured my stomach as Gyrik walked around to the driver's side door and opened it for me. What I felt only had a little bit to do with my driving companion. Most of my nerves were for what I'd see once we headed south.

Repeat was already on my seat, waiting. Gravitating toward the comfort his presence offered, I picked him up and got in. Gyrik walked around the hood of the truck as I gave Repeat some head kisses to soothe myself. It was enough that I could calmly place Repeat on the seat between us once Gyrik got in.

"I usually don't drive with them out like this. If one of them tries to go under my feet or on my lap, we'll need to kennel them."

I'd already had Zach place the small kennel in the back, but I hoped we wouldn't need to use it. Pete and Repeat tended to cry the whole time. Plus, I felt a lot better having them close by me—comforting while I drove, not only with someone who didn't consider himself human but into a rumored to be devastated world.

The truck in front of me rolled forward, and I followed. From the corner of my eye, I saw Gyrik reach to pull Repeat into his lap while holding Pete in his arms.

He seemed to like them, and they had no problem with him,

based on the volume of their purring. All the things I should have been dwelling on last night resurfaced.

"Is it okay if I ask you some questions while we drive?" I asked.

"Yes."

Now that I had permission, I wasn't sure where to start.

"You mentioned brothers. How many of you are there?"

He was quiet for several seconds, and I glanced at him.

"You don't know?"

"I know, but I promised Bram I wouldn't tell anyone that information. He said keeping our numbers secret will help ensure our safety."

I did a double-take at him. "*Your* safety? You lifted that generator into the truck like it weighed nothing."

He turned to look at me, his gaze almost sad.

"Bullets can still kill us. Humans like guns and shooting when they're afraid of something."

So he wasn't trying to be mysterious or shifty, just trying to protect himself. It made me feel a little bad for him and also a little safer knowing he wasn't invincible.

"Have you been shot at a lot?"

His expression morphed as he chuckled. "Yes. Many, many times. It's a good thing I can move fast."

He kind of looked cute when he was smiling.

"Really? You can dodge bullets?"

"Sometimes."

"What else can you do that a human can't?"

CHAPTER SIX

GYRIK

My thoughts immediately shifted to what I'd learned from my brothers, but Angel's warnings stopped me from telling Ava I could release inside of her repeatedly without going soft like a human male.

"I can jump higher than a human can."

"Really? How high?"

"I could jump from the ground to your cabin's roof without strain. Higher, too."

"Higher than your brothers?"

Ava wanted to know more about *me*. She was *interested*. I tried to hide my excitement, but Repeat lifted his head to stare at me when my cock twitched under him again. I petted him and silently begged him not to move.

Ava had looked so lost and afraid when she'd asked if she would be hurt if she left with us. I didn't want her to think I had only asked her to return with us so we could have sex.

"Most of them. I can also hear better. When Pete and Repeat aren't purring so loudly, I can hear your heartbeat."

"Wow. So…faster, stronger, better hearing, and immune to getting sick?"

"Yes."

"I can see why some humans don't like you," she said.

My hope shriveled inside of me.

"Especially human men. Based on my experience, most of them can't handle being shown up by someone—male or female. It's sad, really. I think of all the female friends I've had who've cheered me on to do more and be more, and I can't imagine living a life where I didn't have that support. A life filled with thinking I'm competing against everyone or everyone's competing against me just sounds exhausting."

She flashed me a smile that melted my insides.

"Don't get me wrong. I can be competitive, too. But it's not all the time. I don't feel an ever-present need to prove myself."

"You think human males do?" I asked.

"Oh yeah. Definitely.

"There was this dick at work who liked putting me down. That's why I was at the cabin. To prove that I was better than him."

A male had pushed Ava down with his dick? I remained very still so she wouldn't know how angry that made me. Pete and Repeat knew. Their ears flicked in my direction even when they didn't look at me.

If Ava had a bad experience with dicks, would she become sad like May? I didn't want her to be afraid of them. Of me.

"He won't ever hurt you again," I said when I could speak without sounding angry.

"Oh, I never let him hurt me. He was just an annoying ass."

Could a male's ass be annoying? I frowned, wondering if this was one of those miscommunication moments that Angel often mentioned to us.

"How long ago were the cities bombed?" she asked.

"Almost five months now."

She sighed as she followed the truck in front of us around the bend in her road.

"I can't believe I didn't notice something like that. Is there any chance my family is still alive?"

She wasn't the first survivor who'd asked that question this trip. So I gave her the answer I heard Bram give the others.

"It's impossible to say right now with our limited ability to communicate over any significant distance, but it's part of why we're out here. We're noting the names of the people we find and marking our maps. We won't give locations away, but if someone in the future asks about a certain name in a certain area, maybe we'll have an answer."

"Wow. That's really…nice."

I nodded. "I am not the kind of male who will push you down with my dick."

She made a little sound and glanced at me with visible surprise.

"I won't push you down with any part of me. Ever," I promised.

"Um. Okay. Thanks, I guess? What cities have you been through? My sister's name is Kylie. She was living with my mom, Stacy, and helping care for our grandpa, Charlie, in the Shakopee area, southwest of Minneapolis, a big city south of here."

"We've avoided all the big cities. The bombing makes them hard to navigate with the trucks, and the remaining infected make them unsafe to travel without the trucks. But your family was probably evacuated with everyone else."

"Yeah, I guessed that already, but I was still kind of hoping you've heard of them."

I hated seeing her sadness, so I said, "There is a woman named Stacy at Tenacity. But Bram said it's common for humans to have the same name."

"So don't get my hopes up, right?"

"Angel says that hope keeps people alive."

"Angel sounds pretty smart."

"She is. She just had a baby. Daisy is perfect. She's smaller than Pete and lies still like Repeat when she's held."

Ava glanced at Pete in my arms, then at me.

"You like kids?"

"Yes. My brothers and I never saw any before coming to the surface."

"Never? Didn't you say you were reborn in your world whenever you removed heads?"

"Yes. We were reborn in the waters but exactly as we are. Only, without any hair." I reached up and rubbed my hand over my shorter hair.

"You know, the more I learn, the weirder this all sounds," she said.

"Mya didn't believe many things at first either. When you meet her, you should ask her about watching our rebirth."

"I think I might have to do that."

Ava's questions didn't end there. She asked about the world I'd known before coming to the surface. She seemed very interested in the animals who had lived in the caves with us and was sad to learn that many of the animals on the surface had run away and were hard to find now.

I carefully asked questions of my own, avoiding the ones I knew I shouldn't ask—like asking what her pussy tasted like or if she had a boyfriend or husband. Instead, I asked about where she grew up and what work she did before she went to the cabin. Emily, another woman in Tolerance who was helping my brothers and me find females of our own, said those were safe questions. Ava responded well to both.

My fascination with her grew the longer we talked. She was funny and smart and interesting. I learned she'd been living independently for years. She hadn't dated seriously, which meant she had no boyfriend or husband. I tried to think of a question that would lead her to admit the flavor of her pussy.

The radio crackled.

"Are there any homes Ava wants us to check before we leave Silver Bay?" Will asked.

"I didn't really know anyone from around here."

I relayed that to Will then leaned forward to look up at the sky before speaking on the radio again.

"It looks like it will snow soon."

"We'll let you know when we need you in front," he responded.

"What did he mean by needing you in front?"

"New snow will make it harder to see where the road is. I'll run ahead of the truck to ensure Will doesn't drive off the road."

"Why you?"

"I don't get cold like humans do."

She glanced at my shirt. "I guess not. What did you do before coming here? Not to this area but here on the surface?"

I talked about the fields, the things we made like the pants and boots I wore, and how we'd honed our fighting skills to defend ourselves against the hounds.

"I think I'd like to see a challenge," she said. "It sounds interesting."

The idea of Ava wanting to watch me spar with one of my brothers sent a thrill through me. Repeat lifted his head to look at me, and I tried to will my throbbing cock into a relaxed state—an impossibility with Ava's sweet scent filling the cab.

"If we're worried about losing the road, why aren't we taking the main highway?" Ava asked after it started snowing.

"This way will take us around Duluth," I said. "The highway would take us directly into it."

"Gotcha." She sucked her lower lip into her mouth, and Repeat got off my lap to lie next to me. I quickly set Pete there to cover my reaction to what she was doing to her mouth.

"Is there any chance we can check my family's house?" she asked after a moment. "I just need to know if they left a message for me like the people did in that house in Silver Bay. If you have a map, I can show you where it is."

I was willing to search any home she wanted, but I knew better than to promise to check *her* home, especially if it was still in the city.

"When we stop, I'll ask Bram to show you the maps we have."

"Thank you, Gyrik. So much. I know that's not a 'yes,' but it wasn't a 'no' either, and I appreciate that."

THANK YOU, Gyrik.

I grinned as her pretty words of thanks repeated in my mind.

The snow was getting deeper as it fell thickly from the sky, and I could no longer see our tracks from the day before, but that didn't matter. The dips on the side of the road made it easy enough to find the center.

I knew Bram was having difficulty navigating, though, despite my presence a hundred feet ahead of him, when he flashed his lights.

Pivoting, I ran backward to wave for him to stop then sprinted past their truck to check on Ava and Zach. I hadn't liked leaving Zach with her, but I hadn't wanted her to drive alone, either.

Since Zach had promised me weeks ago that he had no interest in women older than himself, I knew he was the safest of the three to put with Ava.

Ava rolled down the window when she saw me approach.

"Something wrong?" she asked.

"It's getting too hard to see, and I don't think the snow will stop soon. I'll find a house for us and take you there. Stay inside with Zach until I come back."

I glanced at Zach, not liking that he needed to stay despite his promise.

He grinned at me. "Don't worry. I'm being helpful and telling Ava all about you and your brothers."

That didn't reassure me. Zach thought everything was funny, and I wasn't sure what stories he was telling. He wouldn't tell her about our desperation for women, would he?

"That's the blink I was talking about," Zach said. "It means he's either confused or not sure how to answer. You can ask what's wrong or just offer more of an explanation to see if that clears things up. It usually does." He looked at me. "See? I'm helpful."

I grunted, and as I turned away, I heard him say, "That's like an agree to disagree in most cases."

When I glanced back, her window was up, and they were still talking. Perhaps Zach was being helpful, but I still didn't want to give up any more time with her than necessary. So I sprinted away from the vehicles and watched for an opening off the road that might indicate a driveway.

I found a home several minutes later.

The locked door was a good sign. I walked through the cold rooms and noted the undisturbed state of everything as I checked all the usual hiding places. Since the smart ones had died a few weeks ago, the infected didn't hide anymore. They still responded to sound, though, and sometimes light. So, I didn't move quietly.

As soon as I verified the house was safe, I returned to lead the vehicles back to it. While they parked, I watched Ava, anticipating spending the rest of the day with her.

She was looking at the house as she turned off the engine and gathered Pete in her arms. I jogged over and tapped on her window.

"It is safe to go inside," I said when she looked at me.

She nodded, and Zach gave me a thumbs-up before motioning that I should leave.

Don't let your desperation show.

Rather than stay with her like I wanted, I jogged to the main truck and helped Will dig out our overnight supplies.

"Here," he said, handing over the first tote.

Ava and Zach were a few steps behind me with her cats as I went inside with it.

"Is this what you normally do?" Ava asked. "Break into vacant houses?"

"Pretty much," Zach said. "It's warmer than sleeping outside, but if we have to, we have the gear to do that too. We did last night."

She glanced from me to the tote I carried. "Do you need help with anything?"

"Yeah," Zach said as I set the tote on the kitchen table. "You can help me see if we can get the heat and water going. Let's check the basement."

"Wait," I said.

Although I'd already walked through it, I didn't want Ava down there with only Zach. He could defend himself, but what about her?

"Actually, why don't you help her, Gyrik?" Zach asked, reading the situation well. "I'll carry in supplies."

He walked out without waiting for an answer from either of us.

CHAPTER SEVEN

AVA

GYRIK WAS COVERED IN SNOW FROM HIS TIME OUTSIDE, AND IT WASN'T melting off.

With Zach's stories running through my head about how Gyrik and his brothers had been mistreated by the people in their survivor colonies, I reached up and gently brushed the snow off Gyrik's shoulders. Then I motioned for him to lean down.

He did so with startling speed, proving he hadn't exaggerated that talent. I flashed a half-smile at him, hoping he couldn't hear how it'd made my heart race, and brushed the snow from the top of his head.

"You looked like you were part snowman," I said. "I'm actually surprised it's snowing like this so late in the season."

Will entered with a tote and said, "We weren't expecting this much snow on the ground either. Back in Missouri, it's starting to feel like spring."

"It was like that here a few weeks ago. The lake likes to throw some unexpected snow, though."

He nodded, and while he set the tote on the table, I glanced at Gyrik. "Ready to see if we can turn on the heat?"

He led the way to the basement and explained the rules for entering unknown spaces. Move quietly and listen. Stay close to him at all times. Say if I see anything suspicious—like if things were moved that might seem out of place. Trust him to keep me safe.

Basements had never bothered me before, but his warnings put me on edge despite not having seen anyone infected with any sickness. When we found the furnace, the pilot light was out, and the valve on the gas line was closed. A long lighter waited on top of the furnace.

"I think we're in business," I said.

A few minutes later, the pilot was lit, and I heard the furnace kick in.

"No way!" Zach shouted from above.

The water heater was the same as the furnace.

"I think whoever lived here planned on coming back," I said.

Gyrik grunted.

"You don't think they will?"

"I hope they do, but I do not think they will," he said.

He sounded sad about it, which made me sad even though I still had a hard time believing that many people had died. I would have been in complete denial if I hadn't seen Silver Bay for myself.

Bram was already heating something for lunch on the stove when we returned to the kitchen. Zach sat at the table with a board game.

"Are you ready to waste some time?" he asked.

It'd been ages since I had played any board game, and I quickly agreed.

We ate lunch and played games as the snow fell heavily outside. Gyrik left occasionally. The others explained he was checking the area to ensure the lights and noise weren't attracting any infected. However, based on the amount of snow covering Gyrik every time he returned, I doubted the light and sound from the house carried beyond the immediate area.

Before dinner, Bram pulled out the map to plan their route for the next day. He pointed to where he thought we were, a section of Highway 23 south of Duluth, then brought out a spiral-bound book with all the states in it to show me where we were going.

"Is there any chance we could check Shakopee?" I asked. "It's a little out of the way, but not more than a few hours."

Will and Bram shared a look.

"I already know my family won't be there," I said. "I'm just hoping they might have left a message for me."

They exchanged another glance.

"I need subtitles for these looks you're giving each other," I said.

"They're worried about what will happen if your family *is* still there," Zach said. "Right now, ignorance can give you hope. That might be taken away from you if we go there."

I understood what he wasn't saying. They were worried I'd lose my grip on my sanity if I saw my family sick. And that added another notch of fear. Zach had tried to prepare me for what I might see.

Zombies, just like in the movies.

I'd heard him, but my doubt lingered. I was just like that, though, having a hard time believing what I couldn't see.

"For some people, ignorance would be bliss. For me, the unknowns are hell. I closed myself off from the world, and it fell apart without me even knowing it. Now I need to know what that ignorance actually cost me."

Zach reached out and patted my shoulder. "I hope they aren't there."

I looked from him to the other two. "Does that mean we can check?"

"We will check," Gyrik said.

Bram flipped back to the Minnesota map so I could point to Shakopee. I watched him plot the route, noting all the back roads he was choosing. And the planning didn't stop there. They made backup route plans in case roads were impassible.

"The infected don't make roadblocks anymore, but some of the old ones might still be there. And humans like to make them too to ambush for supplies."

"Great," I said faintly.

The weather let up a few hours after dark. Unfortunately, the heat quit just as we settled in for the night.

"It happens," Bram said. "I think the lines run out of pressure or something. If we shut off the gas, sometimes the pressure can build again, but I think it'd be better to leave it off while we sleep. We'll be gone at first light, anyway."

I shut off the gas first while everyone used the bathroom one last time, then shut off the water and drained the lines so the pipes wouldn't freeze.

When I came back upstairs, Zach explained their routine. They split up in the bedrooms, sleeping in pairs with the door closed and locked.

"Never leave a closed room until Gyrik gives the all clear in case an infected breaks in while we sleep. And keep the lights off at night so the infected aren't drawn in.

"If it's all right with you, the three of us will take the master, and you and Gyrik can take this room. Gyrik will be able to hear through the walls. Oh, and he doesn't need much sleep, so he's fine sitting against the door while you take the bed."

I glanced from Zach to Gyrik and nodded.

After spending the day with them, I felt comfortable enough to sleep in a room with any of them, especially with all the informational tidbits they'd dropped throughout the day. The infected were often silent, and while not as smart as a human, some knew how to work a doorknob…if they still had hands.

Being closed in a room with any of them was better than sleeping alone.

Gyrik followed me into the second room where a cold-weather sleeping bag and Pete and Repeat already waited on the bed. Someone had also moved their litter box and food and water bowls into the room.

"Did I do it right?" Gyrik asked when he caught me looking at their setup.

"You did this?"

His gaze shifted to the food and water bowls as he hesitantly nodded.

"You did great, Gyrik. Thank you."

I sat on the bed and toed off the boots I'd loosened a while ago. That was another nifty little tidbit Will had dropped. Don't take your boots off unless you have to or unless you're somewhere you know you're one hundred percent safe.

Pausing, I looked at Gyrik. "Does this count as a time I can take my boots off?"

He quickly nodded. "You are safe. I promise."

I stripped off my sweater, too, but hesitated when I would have removed my jeans.

"What's wrong?" Gyrik asked, watching me.

"I usually sleep in shorts. Sleeping in jeans probably won't be fun."

"You don't have to sleep in anything."

Zach's entertaining stories about miscommunications ran through my head, and I grinned at Gyrik.

"Sleeping naked might be a little too cold for me."

I watched the tips of Gyrik's ears darken as he stared at me.

"I'm just teasing you, Gyrik. I know you weren't suggesting I sleep naked. But if you promise to make sure nothing will send me running out of this room in my underwear, I don't mind removing my jeans."

He gave me one of the blinks Zach warned me about and a jerky nod, so I figured it was okay. I didn't hate jeans, and I understood why Will had suggested I wear them—to better protect against bites—but I really didn't want to have to sleep in them if I didn't have to.

Once I settled into the sleeping bag with Pete and Repeat snuggled around me, I told Gyrik he could turn down the small lantern he'd brought in with him. In the dark, I listened to him settle in front of the door.

"Zach told me a little about what life's been like for you and your brothers. Do you ever get time to relax? Even while playing games, I saw how you kept glancing at the windows."

"Yes, I relax." His voice was slow and deep in the darkness. Soothing.

"How?"

He started talking about how he walked around and watched the kids play in his community or talked with his brothers or went to the other community to see if he could help with anything. While I wouldn't have found any of that relaxing, that *he did* spoke of the kind of person he was. Craving connection and involvement. A man not afraid of pitching in wherever, however.

Lonely.

"You've mentioned a few women today. Are you dating any of them?" I asked.

"No, I am single."

I smiled into the darkness at the way he said it—like he was worried I'd misunderstand. Only someone with zero social awareness would have missed how he'd been watching me throughout the day. It hadn't bothered me, though. After listening to Zach's stories, I'd understood Gyrik's attention, laced with a hint of fascination. I'd be fascinated, too, if I'd never seen a man before. Gyrik's attention was flattering, honestly. But only because he wasn't creepy about it. More like shy and apologetic. It was cute.

"Can I ask you some personal questions?" I asked.

"Yes."

"You don't have to answer anything that makes you feel uncomfortable. I'm just curious how far you've gone with a woman."

I could imagine his blink in the silence that followed.

"How far?" he said finally.

"Yeah."

"Several have gone on supplies runs with us. We never stay out longer than a single day, though. So, I think maybe twenty miles."

I ducked my face into Pete's back to smother my humor. When I knew I wouldn't laugh, I lifted my head and clarified.

"Have you ever held a woman's hand?"

"No."

"Hugged one?"

"I hugged you."

"Anyone before me?"

"I've carried one. Does that count?"

"Not really."

"I'm sorry," he said.

"Don't be. Those are great answers. Good night, Gyrik."

"Good night, Ava. Sleep well. You are safe. I promise."

I closed my eyes and listened to Pete and Repeat's low purrs, grateful they weren't my only companions tonight.

AT SOME POINT during the night, the meager heat the house had accumulated from the few hours the furnace had run slowly bled away. The sleeping bag, which had started out uncomfortably warm, wasn't enough to keep me warm, thanks to how I'd unzipped it to sprawl out.

I reached back to pull my underwear out of my crack then tugged the sleeping bag out from under Pete and Repeat.

"Are you cold?" Gyrik asked from the darkness.

I jumped, having forgotten for a moment where I was and that I wasn't alone. Thankfully, it was dark, and he hadn't witnessed me de-thonging my underwear.

"Yeah," I said. "Sorry for waking you up."

"I wasn't sleeping."

I heard him move, and I was plucked off the bed a second later. Startled, I grabbed onto Gyrik's shoulders as he supported all my weight with one arm and used the other to straighten out the sleeping bag on the bed.

Gyrik radiated heat as he set me down again. His hands skimmed over my legs, tucking them into the sleeping bag before zipping me up. It happened so fast that I didn't even register his touch until it was gone.

Shivering, I huddled in the sleeping bag, rubbing my legs together to warm them.

"Better?" he asked.

"Not really. I should probably put my pants on again."

CHAPTER EIGHT

GYRIK

"No," I said quickly.

Watching the thin material of her underwear slowly disappear between the rounded globes of her backside had been torture. The lingering sensation of her softness in my palms was killing me. I didn't want her more covered. I wanted her less covered.

Palming my erection in the darkness, I cleared my throat to remove my desperation.

"You said they aren't comfortable," I said. "If I lie next to you, it should help warm you faster."

Pete watched me, his stare slightly condemning as I waited for her response.

"Sure. I'm willing. Get over here."

My pulse skipped and sped up in anticipation. I carefully moved her closer to the wall and eased my weight onto the bed.

"You're not going to unzip the sleeping bag?" she asked.

"If I do, the heat will escape."

"What heat? I need yours because I don't have any of my own."

She wanted to feel me next to her? Panic and need kept me frozen in place.

I listened to the rasp of the zipper and fought not to groan as she lifted my arm and positioned herself against my side. The way she wrapped her arm around my waist and the feel of her soft body against mine unmade me. I barely breathed, afraid of startling her away.

"How are you so warm?" she asked, her voice muffled by my side and the sleeping bag she'd tugged over her head.

She wiggled closer, and I felt the weight of her leg settle over mine. I itched to touch her but kept my hands where they were on the mattress, letting her choose how to warm herself.

"Are you okay with this?" she asked.

"Yes." I hoped the word only sounded pained to my ears and not hers.

"If I make you uncomfortable, just push me away."

I would have rather let one of the infected slowly chew off my arm than push her soft body away from mine. If she wanted to use me as a bed, I would happily hold her all night long.

The image of her underwear slowly creeping along her dimpled skin as she restlessly moved on top of me played through my mind, and I bit my lip to stop myself from groaning.

Her breathing slowed as her hand warmed on my stomach.

I closed my eyes and focused on the feel of her against me. Her sweet scent filled my nose with each breath. Her fingers twitched against my chest.

Nothing could tear me from this bed.

"Do you think they're awake yet?" Zach asked.

My gaze shifted to the door, and I silently willed the pair outside of it to go away.

Bram had been the first one to leave their room and was checking the house for infected. Will and Zach had stayed behind to wait for the all-clear and to ensure nothing approached Ava's room. They knew how important she was to me. To my brothers.

Farther away, I could hear Bram searching, but I knew he

wouldn't find anything. The house had remained quiet the whole night.

"I'm guessing Gyrik's awake," Will said. "And he probably doesn't want us knocking on that door until they come out on their own."

I could hear the humor in his words but hoped he would still keep Zach from interrupting.

Ava had used me as a pillow the entire night. I had a wet spot on my chest. Pete was wedged between my legs, hot boxing my testicles, which was probably the only thing stopping them from throbbing painfully from a night of Ava's restless movements against me. Repeat had already eaten and defecated in the litter a few seconds ago. The scent of Ava's hair, which was currently covering the entirety of my face, was mostly filtering out the smell.

Between the cats and Ava, I hadn't moved for hours. I didn't want to disturb her.

"A word to the wise, Gyrik," Will said from the hallway. "If Ava's drooling on you or her hair is messy, you'll want to slip out of there *before* she wakes up, or she'll be embarrassed and try to avoid you for at least half the day."

I frowned through her hair and wondered if wearing it like a mask counted as messy.

Deciding not to risk it, I carefully removed Pete from his place. He made unhappy sounds. I understood how he felt as I eased out from Ava's arms.

Standing beside the bed, I watched her move restlessly for a moment before settling again. The ache I'd been fighting the entire night intensified as her underwear shifted over her backside, showing me the full expanse of her rounded flesh. I wanted to touch her. Feel her softness.

My fingers twitched as I reached for her. At the last second, I grabbed the sleeping bag to cover her before reluctantly turning away.

When I opened the door, Zach grinned at me and pointed at the wet spot on my shirt.

"Good call to leave," he said softly. "They get embarrassed by that."

"Why?" I asked, already moving toward the living room.

"Not everyone likes to be drooled on, I guess," Will said with a shrug.

What male wouldn't want a female's mouth juices on him? All of the ways my brothers had described experiencing their female's mouth on their bodies vividly played through my mind as we joined Bram.

Ava appeared dressed—unfortunately—a few minutes after the morning stew started simmering.

"Good morning." She smiled at everyone as she picked up Pete. Then, her gaze settled on me. "Did I hog the bed?"

"No," I said, understanding that term. She'd taken up just the right amount of space in the bed and on me.

She approached where I stood by the stove and looked into the pot.

"Are you hungry?" I asked.

"I am. Stew's an unusual choice for breakfast."

"You'll find that we don't stick to food norms in the communities," Bram said. "We're just grateful for whatever food we have."

Ava faced Bram. "I'm sorry. My comment wasn't meant to sound judgmental. I was just curious."

"I know," Bram said. "You were well stocked and still have plenty of the breakfast-type foods you're used to. We can make them if you want. The stew is just something that will feed us all."

She glanced at Zach and then at me. "Sorry. I forgot you lean toward meats."

"You have nothing to apologize for," I said. "I know what it's like to learn the rules of a new world. It's confusing at first."

Her soft smile warmed me from the inside, and I turned back to the stove so she wouldn't see how much I liked her attention.

After we ate, we packed up and headed out. With so much snow on the roads, I had to run ahead again. But by lunch, we'd moved far enough to the south that I didn't need to run out front anymore, and I sat comfortably in Ava's truck with Pete and Repeat on my lap.

"It's weird to drive so long and not see another car. It's been a day already without seeing another person on the road. Not even a track." She sighed. "It's not that I didn't believe what you were saying...I just think the reality of it is still settling in, you know?"

I did know. It'd been like that for me when I'd first come to the surface. The sun, which was still bright to me now, even behind the clouds, had felt like a hundred bone needles piercing my eyes. The people had been strange and angry. Everything I'd done and said had been wrong. I'd mumbled thousands of apologies for misunderstandings the first few weeks we'd lived with the humans. Yet, I loved this world and the brightness and the people. It was better than the endless loneliness of the caves.

The radio clicked, and Zach started to speak. "We're stopping. Ava, cut the engine as soon as you're parked. Gyrik, we need you up front."

"What's happening?" Ava asked, slowing.

"I'll find out," Gyrik said. "Stay here, and lock the doors."

I waited until I heard the door lock behind me to jog to the lead truck.

"Are you low on fuel?" I asked as Bram rolled down the window.

"Yeah, that's part of the reason we stopped. The other is that." He pointed down the road to one of the big buildings that often had supplies. "Elk River is bigger than I thought to have one of those stores. With the extra room in Ava's truck, I'm tempted to check it for supplies."

I jumped on top of the truck and squatted low to study the building for a few minutes. Nothing moved in the parking lot. I scanned the road and didn't see any tracks either. Yet, something told me the store wasn't worth our time.

Landing softly beside the door, I said as much to Bram.

"Then we won't. But I have a feeling you're going to be needed ahead. I think it'll be safer for us if you ride on top until we're clear of the city. Zach should drive the truck for Ava. She's never seen an infected yet, and we can't afford for her to panic and drive off the road."

I agreed and jogged around to the passenger side for Zach to join me. We refueled the vehicles with the spare containers in the back with the generator. When we finished, he clapped me on the back.

"Don't worry," he said. "I'll keep her safe for you.".

"Keep yourself safe, too," I said. "Uan will make me wish for rebirth if anything happens to you."

Zach grinned, and as we approached, he motioned for Ava to get out of the truck. She did so with a look of question on her pretty face.

"What's up?"

"We're switching," Zach said. "You get shotgun for a while."

"Why?"

"I have my zombie driving license, and you don't."

Her gaze shifted to the area around us. "Really?"

"I get it," Zach said. "You're more curious than afraid right now, but that'll probably change the first time you see one. And I think we'll see a few."

He glanced at me, and I nodded. She saw that, and I watched how her hands moved in her coat pockets. She was afraid, and I hated that. But fear would make her more cautious, and caution would keep her alive.

"Come," I said, holding out my hand.

Her bare fingers clasped mine as I led her to the passenger side.

"There are rules when driving through infected," I said. "Don't slow down. Keep a steady speed. Use your wipers if you can't see. Don't stop. If anything happens and you do stop, call my name. I'll hear you. Don't leave the vehicle. Don't roll down your window. Do you understand?"

She nodded jerkily.

"If you need to go to the bathroom, I recommend going now," Zach said when I opened the door for her. "The questionability of bladder control is no joke the first time you see one."

She looked from him to me and back again before quietly admitting she needed to go.

I stood guard as she squatted behind the truck. Zach was in the cab talking to Bram over the radio. They were worried about Ava's reaction. So was I. I didn't want her to fear this world. I'd seen how fear could slowly erode a human's will to live, and I didn't want that for Ava. She smiled and laughed and cuddled. She was perfect the way she was, and I didn't want that to change.

But I also wanted her to live.

When she finished, I walked her to the door and watched her buckle in.

"Bram said to remind you that you can change your mind at any time," Zach said. "About checking your home."

Ava nodded and looked at me. "Where are you going to be?"

"On top of the truck, watching. I'll jump down and run ahead to clear the way if I see anything. Follow the rules, and you'll be safe. I promise."

She nodded, and I closed the door.

Once Zach started the truck and gave me a thumbs up, I jumped to the roof of Bram's truck and thumped on it twice. It eased forward, and I nervously glanced back at Ava.

Something told me passing through Elk River wouldn't be easy on her.

CHAPTER NINE

AVA

"I can't believe he can jump like that," I said, watching Gyrik squat atop the lead truck.

"That's nothing. He could jump to the top of that building with no problem."

I looked where Zach was pointing and felt another wave of awe. Sure, Gyrik had said as much, but seeing was believing. And Gyrik was more able than I'd imagined. Faster than I'd guessed. Stronger. And a fantastic snuggler. Considerate too.

The last man I'd seriously dated had been a narcissist. I had seen his love bombing for what it was within six months, and I had broken up with him. Unfortunately, that hadn't been the end. I'd had to deal with the fallout for months afterward until he'd moved on to another woman. After that, I'd been standoffish about attempting another relationship. It'd left a mark on me, making it hard to trust any overtures of affection.

However, that's not how it felt with Gyrik. He did things quietly, without any demands for recognition. While packing up, he'd cleared the snow off my truck, carried the cats and all their supplies out, and made sure that my water bottle was full. I'd had to ask to find out who did those things. And when I thanked him, he'd downplayed his actions, again not looking for recognition. It felt…right. Normal.

But was it affection or just kindness?

The way he looked at me as he glanced back from his perch felt like it was more than just kindness. Maybe that was just wishful thinking, though. Or desperation.

In the last twenty-four hours, I'd heard from each man that Gyrik was the one who'd keep us safe…and I believed them. He was so different, not just in appearance but in everything about him. While he seemed nice enough, I also recognized he wasn't someone I would ever want mad at me.

Then, was my budding interest in him because of actual attraction or self-preservation?

"Zach, take the center so I can take the tail," Will said over the radio.

"Copy that," I said back.

Zach eased back from the truck in front of us while Will moved to the side. Once Zach edged by him and we were in the middle, Zach closed the distance between us and Bram's truck. I glanced back to see Will doing the same.

"Yesterday, you mentioned that you're a programmer. What kind of stuff can you program? Any games?"

Zach's question distracted me for the next few minutes and eased the tension that had crept in. He seemed pretty carefree when speaking, but the things he said and the observations he made showed he wasn't the typical devil-may-care teen.

Which was probably why he didn't run us into the ditch when the first infected appeared, shambling through the snow.

Zach hadn't exaggerated. She was exactly like every zombie depiction Hollywood ever came up with. She looked about my age but with discolored, decaying skin, cloudy eyes, and dirty, tattered clothes.

Her long hair hung in icicles around her head, and she could barely move through the snow. Not that it was deep. It looked more like she was having trouble getting her limbs to work.

The way her head tracked the sound of our vehicles as she struggled to move was disturbing.

Gyrik jumped down from the top of the truck, glanced at me, and mimed covering my eyes.

"He doesn't want you to watch," Zach said.

"Yeah," I said faintly. "Got it."

I closed my eyes and focused on breathing instead of crying.

The apocalypse was real.

Bites.

Sickness.

Zombies.

And I'd hidden away from the worst of it. Guilt hit me hard, and I thought of my family.

What if what I just saw had happened to Mom, Pops, and Kylie? What if I found them in the house like that?

Bram's assurance that I could change my mind made more sense. Would I be able to deal with seeing my family like that? Worse, would I be able to deal with what would need to be done? The men had stressed several times how dangerous the infected still were…how there were still so many left.

The rules Zach had already shared, like the ways to kill an infected, ran through my mind.

"Gyrik removed her head, didn't he?" My words were barely audible over the hum of the engine, but Zach heard.

"Yeah. He has to. Leaving them as they are means they'll be there to hurt the humans that are still alive."

I nodded and leaned my head back against the seat.

"You should keep your eyes closed."

"I will, but we both know I'll need to face this eventually."

"Aren't you already? Give yourself time to process what you've seen before you add anything more. And there will be more. A lot more. But like I said before, at least, these ones are slower and less scary than what was out there before. Seriously, I don't understand how you made it without anything finding you until now."

"Same."

I'd gotten so lucky. Hopefully, that luck would last a little longer, and I'd find my family holed up and safe. Yet, a thread of doubt remained. My family had known where I was. If they'd had the chance, wouldn't they have tried driving to the cabin to get me, too?

"If you're not busy dodging dead people, can I ask questions?"

"No dodging. Gyrik is keeping them all away. It's easier to clean him than the vehicles. What's your question?"

The image Zach had just painted muted me for an extra few seconds.

"How fast did everything happen? From the time people started being affected to the time the evacuations started?"

"Hours. The bombings happened within days. Everything was chaos. I'm glad you missed it. I still have nightmares about those first few days." He made a derisive sound. "The first few weeks, really. We got smarter. But so did they."

"Do you have any family left?"

"I do. My mom and my sister. My dad's gone."

"I'm sorry."

Pete, who was sleeping in my lap, made an inquisitive sound and started purring as I petted him.

"It is what it is," Zach said. "It's better to accept the circumstances than live in denial. Better chance of survival, you know?"

I nodded and opened my eyes, staring at the cab's ceiling for a moment before turning my head and looking out the window. We were passing through a residential area. Several of the infected people were trying to reach us, but they moved like the first woman had—as if their limbs weren't cooperating with them.

It gave Gyrik time to run to them, one by one. I didn't watch what he was doing, but I glanced behind us and saw how he was throwing the bodies into little piles. My stomach didn't turn. I didn't know why not. It should have.

"Why does he pile them like that?"

"Several reasons that you might find a little nauseating."

"Tell me anyway."

"Well, the body piles used to deter other infected from wandering too close to the area. Those were the smarter ones. We're not sure how smart these ones will get, so the piles are still a warning. But they'll also keep the area neater. There's nothing we can do about the dead right now with the ground frozen, but the scientists stressed how other kinds of sicknesses might become a problem if dead people are just left everywhere."

I hadn't thought of that.

"The day we figured out how to stop the smart ones, they'd surround our community. Hundreds of thousands of infected. More than we could have hoped to kill or keep out once they gathered. They fell where they stood. We're talking miles of dead bodies around the communities.

"It took days to pick them all up and haul them away. Thankfully, it was still cold enough then, or it would have been really bad. We found places to move them to. Some were burned. Some were buried. There were too many to stick to just one method. Hopefully, once the warm weather comes, we won't have any problems."

We continued through Elk River at a steady pace without incident, and I breathed a little sigh of relief when we reached open road. After a few miles, we stopped so Gyrik could wash up.

Not wanting to test my stomach, I didn't look to see why he needed to wash. But I had an imagination and could guess that he was probably covered in the blood of the people he'd beheaded. Rather than be sickened by the thought of it, I was sad for the role he had to play just because he was stronger and immune. I'd glimpsed how he'd had to run from one infected to the next, non-stop, while keeping up with the vehicles. He had to be tired.

"I'll grab his clothes and do a sweep," Zach said over the radio.

"Watch your feet," Bram said in return.

"Stay here," Zach said, handing me the radio.

I kept the cats close so they wouldn't bolt and watched Zach withdraw a handgun I hadn't known he'd been carrying inside his jacket. He glanced at me.

"Sometimes they get caught under the vehicles. Someone died that way. Bitten as they got out. Always make sure someone checks before you get out or jump clear so they can't grab you if they're there."

Without waiting for me to acknowledge the warning, he opened the door and jumped out like he was trying to avoid a puddle. Once he shut the door again, he slowly circled my truck from a safe distance. He did the same to the other two vehicles before climbing into the back of the main one.

I had so much to learn if I wanted to stay alive.

I glanced at Gyrik, who was standing in the middle of a snowy area beside the road. He was shirtless now and using handfuls of snow to clean his skin. Steam rose around him, proof of his warmer body temperature.

Mesmerized, I watched the play of his muscles as he moved, and Pete made another inquisitive sound.

"My thoughts exactly," I said softly.

What exactly was Gyrik? Protector? Alien? Bodybuilder stud muffin? He checked so many boxes that it was hard to tell.

He bent down and pulled off his boots. Barefoot in the snow and completely unbothered by it.

Unable to look away, I watched him reach for his waist. I'd bet my bonus that he wasn't wearing anything else under those leather pants. Did I want him to turn around so I could see? Should I shut my eyes in case he did?

The waistband loosened.

Repeat grumbled, and Pete made little questioning meeps.

Gyrik hooked his fingers in the material at his hips and tugged the molded material down. Inch by sculpted inch, he revealed his glutes.

I think I might be a biter. A nibbler at the bare minimum.

When the leather reached his knees, Gyrik bent slightly to grab the cuff of the pant leg clinging to his calf. The move revealed what hung low between his massively muscular thighs.

He was large all over.

I averted my gaze, and it collided with Zach's, who was watching me from the back of the truck in front of us. He winked at me and hopped down from the truck.

Embarrassed that I was caught perving, a flush ignited in my cheeks.

"Hey, Gyrik. I've got some new clothes for you," he called.

I closed my eyes and rested my head against the back of my seat. Could anyone really blame me for looking? Gyrik wasn't human. Of course, I was curious. It was only natural.

Opening my eyes, I peeked again.

He was still turned away from me. This time, Zach stood beside him, saying things I probably wouldn't like. And Gyrik was listening attentively.

I looked down at Pete and pulled him off my lap to hug him close to my chest.

Will Gyrik be mad that I'd looked? Offended because he just got done killing dozens of people?

Without a doubt, I was the worst person on the planet.

Sighing, I held Pete and started working on how I would word my apology without sounding like a deranged idiot.

Sorry for peeping at your pecker. I didn't actually see much.

Nope.

I didn't mean to look. My eyes slipped.

Funny, but no.

Sorry for watching you change. It's been over a year since I had sex, and I was just making sure I still had a pulse.

I definitely had a pulse; I was just missing my brain at the moment.

Sorry I watched you change. I was so traumatized by seeing my first zombie that I needed something nice to look at.

Actually, that one wasn't too bad.

CHAPTER TEN

GYRIK

ZACH OFTEN SAID THINGS THAT MADE LITTLE SENSE. HE OFTEN FOUND my confusion amusing, which was why I'd agreed to let him join us on the search for survivors. He never got angry and always explained things.

However, I was questioning my wisdom as I tried to understand what he was telling me.

"She wasn't even blinking, Gyrik. Trust me when I say that's a good thing. I think she's starting to have the hots for you."

That I understood—the thought Ava found me physically attractive—and he read the skepticism in my gaze. Holding me for warmth did not mean Ava had the hots for me. Unfortunately.

"I'm starting to feel a little offended here, Gyrik," Zach said. "Have I ever lied to you?"

"No."

"Then why would I lie about this? I'm telling you, she was definitely enjoying the view." He handed me the pile of clothes he held. "Hurry and change so you can go talk to her. I think she's still a little shaken up by the infected, so make sure you drive. Don't worry about me. I'll ride shotgun with Bram."

I watched him jog back toward Bram's truck and glanced at Ava.

She wasn't studying me now. Her head was back on the seat, and her eyes were closed as if she were resting. But a small smile curved her lips. I liked her smile. She looked pretty without it but even prettier with it.

My cock twitched despite the cold temperatures and my numb toes.

Without looking away from Ava, I quickly dressed in grey sweatpants, a black t-shirt, and running shoes. Since clothes that fit me weren't easy to find, I used snow to clean the worst of the blood off my dirty clothes then carried them back to the truck.

Ava didn't open her eyes as I tossed them into the truck's bed, but she did when I opened the driver's side door.

The color in her cheeks darkened as she watched me get in.

"I can drive if you want to take a break," she said.

"I'm not tired. Are you? You had your eyes closed."

She shook her head, and the pink tint coloring her cheeks became more vibrant.

She was watching you, Gyrik. Like…really watching you as you took your pants off. I think she liked what she saw.

Zach was young and hadn't yet experienced the hate and revulsion I had. I could understand why he would think Ava was interested in me if she'd watched me undress. Zach was used to this world already. Ava was not. She saw me removing the heads of the infected for the first time in her life. And witnessed the messy aftermath.

"Are you angry?" I asked.

"Angry?"

"Your face is very red."

The flush spread down her neck. Her heart started to race, and I could see the panic grow in her eyes.

"Some of the females in the community think the way we remove their heads is cruel. It makes them angry."

"Oh. Uh…no, I'm not mad. I would think it's a pretty quick way to go, and I can't imagine they feel very much when they're walking around with other body parts missing."

"Everyone ready?" Zach asked over the radio before I could say anything else.

Ava reached for it too quickly and almost dropped it. She fumbled with it for a second before bringing it to her mouth.

"Ready," she said.

"Ready," Will echoed.

I started the engine and drove for a few minutes as her pulse calmed.

"Zach told you, right?" she asked. "That I saw you change?"

"He did," I said.

"I'm sorry. I wasn't really thinking straight after seeing the infected like that. It was a little traumatizing, you know? The infected, I mean! Not you. You were..." She cleared her throat. "What I'm trying to say is that I wasn't purposely invading your privacy, and I'm sorry that I did."

She was apologizing for looking at me?

I swallowed my offer to change for her again whenever she wanted.

Don't be desperate.

Don't be desperate.

Don't be desperate.

"I'm not angry you saw me without clothes. The way humans always keep themselves covered is something my brothers and I have adapted to.

"When we're reborn, we emerge from the pools without clothes. It's our natural state. Why hide what is natural?" I glanced at her to see if she understood what I was saying and found her staring at me. Had she misunderstood? Did she think I was telling her I would walk naked in front of her?

"I won't remove my clothes in front of you on purpose," I said quickly. "Only to remove infected blood. It's dangerous to humans, and I don't know if Pete and Repeat can be hurt by it either." Repeat was worming his way onto my lap. "I don't want to hurt any of you." I petted him until he settled comfortably.

"I'm not upset you were naked," Ava said. "I felt bad you had to clean up in the snow—that had to be cold. And I feel bad you're the one who has to kill the infected. If it were me, I think I'd be a little upset and sad. Mostly sad, really. Even though they aren't healthy people...or maybe even living...they had been living people at one point. Removing their heads has to be a little upsetting."

I'd never thought of them like that. Rather than seeing what they'd been, I only saw what they were, which was a threat to the healthy humans that remained. A threat to friends like Will, Bram, and Zach and precious females like Ava. But Zach once told me females liked men who could touch their feelings—not just their sex feelings. I tried to think of something full of feelings to say to her.

"It is sad that so many humans were infected before my brothers and I understood what was happening. But only seeing the sadness of what has already happened will blind us to the hope and beauty of what can still happen. That's what Mary says."

"Who's Mary?" Ava asked.

"She is James' wife. They are the oldest people in the communities. Emily says we should listen to them because they have a lifetime of wisdom. Mary isn't afraid to look at us naked. James doesn't let her do it often, though. He says too much is not good for their hearts."

Ava made a choking sound. I glanced at her. She was staring straight ahead.

"I have so many questions," she said quietly.

"You can ask any of them."

For the next hour, I told her about Tolerance and the people who lived there. Stories of Mary and James and the fighting club that Hannah called feight club especially entertained Ava.

"I think that's something I'm going to want to see for myself," she said after I'd described the sacrificial pile of human male penises Hannah and Brenna liked to shoot at.

Although Angel had promised that Hannah didn't hate real

penises or the men attached to them, several of my brothers were still nervous around her when she held a bow. She seemed to enjoy shooting at the replicas very much. I worried Ava might also grow fascinated with them.

"Do you want to shoot at male parts too?" I asked, feeling a hint of concern.

"It sounds like it could be fun."

My concern grew.

"Brooke likes to draw Solin's male parts. That could be fun, too."

"I can't tell if you're offering to show me your parts or trying to dissuade me from joining in the fun of shooting at fake man parts."

"Both?"

Ava laughed. The sound filled the truck and my heart.

"We're stopping here," Zach said over the radio.

"Why are we stopping?" Ava replied.

"It's difficult to drive into the cities that were bombed. It'll be safer for us to wait here while you check your family's home."

"Okay," Ava said as I stopped.

I set Pete on the seat beside me and got out to open her door for her. She exited with Repeat in her arms. I gently stole him, whispered we would return quickly, and put him back in the warm cab.

"Are you sure you want to go in there?" Bram asked, joining us.

Ava looked from him to me. "I'm not sure what going in there entails, so why don't you spell it out for me before I decide?"

"Gyrik is going to take you the rest of the way on foot. It's quieter and will draw less attention. He can also go where the trucks can't if the bombs have obliterated the roads."

She looked around at where we'd stopped. Nothing was around the trucks, just an open expanse of road that would make it easy for them to see anything that approached. Easy to be spotted too.

"How far away are we?" Ava asked.

"The two-twelve is ahead. So, seven or eight miles out from Shakopee. Once you get in there, Gyrik will need you to tell him which way to go. Sound can carry a fair distance on a still day like today. And the snow's not as deep here to slow the infected down."

"It's still cold, though," Will said, joining us. "They move a little slower when they're cold."

"So every time I say anything to him, it will attract infected." Ava looked at me. "What do you think? Am I risking everyone's safety by wanting to go in there?"

I liked that she was looking at me for confirmation.

"It is no more of a risk than trying to find other survivors," I said. "I will keep you safe. Bram, Will, and Zach know how to keep themselves safe while we're in there."

"Okay. Then, I do want to check."

Bram spread out a map on the hood of the car. "We're about here. You probably know the area better than I do, but according to this, there are two bridges that may or may not still be standing to get you across the river. Where's the house again?"

Ava pointed to a location on the map. "In here."

They talked for several minutes about alternate routes and what to do if we met other people. I watched her expression as Bram explained what to do. She was focused, paying close attention to every caution he gave her.

"Not everyone will welcome Gyrik like you did," Bram said. "Expect bullets first and words later. He'll run, find somewhere safe for you, and go back to disarm them. If that happens, stay put. He'll be back for you. And if, for some reason, he doesn't come back, *we* will if we can. Remember the rules. No light and stay quiet at night."

I could see her worry as she nodded and tucked her covered hands under her arms. Was she cold or afraid? I wasn't sure.

"Any questions?" Bram asked.

She shook her head, and he looked at me.

"Watch for anyone following our tracks," I said. "You're in the open. If you need to leave, leave. I'll track you."

"We will. Hurry up so we don't worry." Bram clapped me on the back then got into Ava's truck.

Ava turned toward me, and my palms started to sweat.

Since leaving her bed this morning, I'd been looking forward to holding her soft body against mine again. I imagined her naked against me. No shirt and no underwear. Just skin against skin.

"Are you okay?" Ava asked.

I blinked myself back to the moment and her pretty, amused smile.

"It looked like I lost you there for a second."

"You will never lose me. I promise."

Her smile grew. "You might if we have to run. I saw how fast you can move. There's no way I could keep up with you. Are you ready to start walking?"

I wiped my palms against my legs. "Can I carry you? It will be faster."

"Are you sure? I mean, I know you're strong enough, but it's eight miles."

"I'm sure."

She stretched her arms out from her sides. "Have at it, then."

I had her in my arms a second later and fought not to rub against her like Pete did.

CHAPTER ELEVEN

AVA

BEING LIFTED SO QUICKLY STARTLED A SQUEAK OUT OF ME, AND I grabbed onto Gyrik.

"I wasn't expecting that," I said, looking up at him.

He blinked at me.

Bram's warning that people would shoot Gyrik at first sight made his blink of confusion more endearing. Gyrik didn't look scary enough to shoot at. In fact, he didn't look scary anymore, not even with his cat-like eyes, which were slowly dilating as he studied me.

"You picked me up faster than I'd expected," I explained. "It wasn't bad. Just surprised me."

He grunted and held me more securely as I looked at Bram and gave him a thumbs-up through the windshield.

"You will want to tuck your face against me before I start running," Gyrik said, drawing my attention again.

I looked up at him. "You're going to run with me?"

"Yes. It's faster."

I thought about how he'd run around the vehicles, killing infected, and made a face.

"It's going to be really fast, isn't it?"

"Yes. Tell me if you get cold, and I will stop to warm you."

I glanced at his shirt and nodded. He continued watching me expectantly. Feeling my face heat, I slowly pressed it against his chiseled chest. He was rock solid. I resisted the urge to nuzzle the firmness of his muscles. How was he so incredibly built?

"Thank you for trusting me, Ava," he said before he started moving.

The calm wind probably saved me from immediate frostbite as he ran. As it was, the cold temperature slowly bled the heat from my legs first. When I pressed closer to him, he seemed to know what was wrong because the hand supporting my legs began to roam over my thigh. It helped. How could I be so cold when his exposed hand was still warm?

The thump of his heart near my ear was louder than his breathing and soft footfalls. But not loud enough to drown out the low moan that rang out in the silence.

Chills raced down my spine. Gyrik patted my leg in a reassuring way, not in a "hurry up and look away" way. So, I kept my head down as another moan sounded in a different direction.

It felt like he ran forever before his grip on me tightened.

"Don't scream."

Those softly spoken words were the only warning I had before he jumped, and my stomach did seven somersaults in a row. When he landed, I gagged into his chest. He dropped my legs but didn't push me away like I'd expected. He held me to his chest while rubbing my back.

It was distracting enough that I stopped gagging and focused on the feel of his hand and the numbness in my legs. After a few deep breaths, I lifted my head to look around. We stood on top of the snow-covered flat roof of a building.

He turned me and pointed. On the other side of the Mississippi, across a bridge clogged with cars, a group of infected shambled through the snow. I could tell they were looking for us in the way the group slowly broke apart and went in different directions.

Creepy.

"Which direction?" he asked, his voice low and soft.

Remembering Bram's warning that sound carried, I pointed to the south. Gyrik nodded and took a knee like he meant to tie my shoe. Instead, he started rubbing some warmth back into my legs. I quickly set a hand on his shoulder for balance.

The way he cared for me felt nice, and the break gave me a minute to really look around. Everything was so still. Snow-covered cars were mysterious white lumps on the roads. I didn't see any infected moving around, but I knew they were there now.

I couldn't see anything but distant trees when I looked off toward the cities. Were the buildings gone? Nothing but rubble now?

"Ready?" Gyrik asked.

I held my arms out to him, and he picked me up slowly. Grinning, I looked up at him and pointed south again.

"Ten blocks," I said as softly as possible.

He nodded, walked to the roof's edge, and hugged me close. Taking the hint, I tucked my face against his chest and held my breath so I wouldn't scream as he jumped off the edge.

Going down was less nauseating than jumping upward.

It didn't take long for us to reach the house. Instead of going inside, he nodded toward the dormer's roof, which was less pitched than the rest. Understanding what he meant to do, I shook my head.

He grinned and nodded. He jumped before I could hold my breath, and I felt my stomach turn again. It wasn't as bad as the last time, though. No gagging.

He patted my back as he steadied me.

"Wait here," he said quietly.

He jumped down again. The sound of wood splintering carried through the otherwise quiet area. The responding moan didn't surprise me.

I watched an infected person run forward more swiftly than any previous infected had. His skin, tinged blue from the cold, peeked through his torn and bloody jacket.

He paused in the street, and I watched the way his head slowly lifted to me on the roof. My pulse kicked into overdrive.

In all the rules they'd told me, they'd never said what to do when one spotted you.

Just stay put. Bram said Gyrik would put you somewhere safe. Up high is safe. That guy can't get you up here.

He moaned really loudly. It startled me, and I slipped a little.

Gyrik was next to me a moment later, steadying me.

"More will come. Wait here, then I'll take you inside." He paused, looking from the infected to me. "Do you know him?"

I shook my head and watched Gyrik jump off the roof's edge. The infected just stood there, looking up at me and completely ignoring Gyrik as Gyrik removed his head. Another moan sounded, and Gyrik moved to meet the next infected.

It took several minutes and a body pile between the houses across the street for the infected to stop appearing. Gyrik cleaned himself off, removing his shirt, before returning to help me off the roof.

My stomach churned for a different reason once I was on the ground, facing the door to my childhood home. Gyrik's hand rubbed the back of my jacket.

"We don't need to go in."

But I did need to.

The moment I walked inside, I knew they'd left in a hurry. Pops' blanket was tossed on his chair instead of neatly folded, the way he liked it. The TV remote sat on the middle couch cushion instead of the coffee table as if something had interrupted them while watching a show.

Leaving the living room, I checked the kitchen. The dishes were washed and placed on the drying rack. A pot sat on the stove with a lid on it.

I was so busy looking at the signs of what they'd been doing that I almost missed the note on the table.

We're being evacuated. The soldier said we're going west. After this, it's your turn. Love you. Kylie

A laugh escaped with a tear.

"What does it say?" Gyrik asked.

"They were alive and evacuated west. No location. Just west."

"Molev, our leader, went west. He saw many humans there."

I tucked the note into my pocket and removed the recent family picture from the wall. After ditching the frame, I added the photo to my pocket.

"Is there anything else we should take from here? Anything the community needs? Pops has a shed outback where he keeps his seed catalogs," I added, recalling Zach's mention of a greenhouse.

Gyrik waited until I was once more safely on the roof to check the shed. When he returned, he carried three binders full of seed packets and carefully labeled baggies. He gave them to me to hold while he carried me.

I didn't tuck my face against his chest as he ran back the way we'd come. Rather than taking the same bridge, he followed the trail to the south where the other bridge remained intact as well. Once he crossed over the river, he took the walking trail that edged the water to cut over to a road that led north and successfully avoided all the subdivisions.

It felt like it took a lot longer to return to the trucks than it had to get to the house. But Gyrik didn't look remotely winded when he finally stopped in front of my truck again.

Bram waved from inside the cab and pointed to Repeat, who was doing his impersonation of a fur stole. I grinned and looked up at Gyrik, who hadn't yet set me down. He was studying me intently.

"Are you all right?" I asked.

He nodded and set me down in a way that felt a little reluctant.

Bram got out of the cab and joined us, leaving the cats behind.

"How did it go?" he asked, looking at Gyrik.

"The section of the city we moved through didn't look bombed," Gyrik said.

"Any power on?"

"No," Gyrik said.

"That's too bad. At these temps, the canned goods probably won't make it, but it might be worthwhile to come back for other supplies. What do you have there?" Bram nodded to the binders I held.

"My grandfather's seed collection. Since retiring, he spent a lot of his time gardening. Zach mentioned the greenhouses in Unity, and I thought they might be useful."

Bram nodded and clapped Gyrik on the arm. "I'll get you a shirt."

My gaze drifted over Gyrik's bare chest, which I'd had my face pressed against the entire way back. He really had a nice chest.

After tearing my gaze from the muscle display, I opened the truck door to tuck the binders behind the seat and pet Pete. Repeat hopped out of the truck and high-stepped his way through the snow to Gyrik, calling loudly the whole way.

Gyrik scooped him up and nuzzled Repeat's face with his nose. It was so cute. Bare from the waist up, buff as sin, and loving on a cat.

He glanced up and caught me watching with a dumb smile on my face.

I flushed and looked away as Bram returned with a new shirt and the map. Bram went over the route he wanted to take and asked for my input on towns along the backroad he chose, which pretty much headed straight south, as Gyrik covered himself.

Once we had a plan, Gyrik opened the passenger door for me.

"Are you sure you don't want me to drive after all the running you did? You could take a nap."

His answer was to help me into my seat and set Repeat on my lap.

The next several hours passed rapidly between interesting conversations and the occasional driver switch to navigate through small towns. Gyrik never seemed to get tired or bored. However, by the time he found us a house for the night, he was out of clean clothes.

For Gyrik's sake, I hoped the ranch-style home with solar panels would have heat and running water.

We followed the previous day's routine. While the others carried in supplies, I went to the basement with Gyrik and tried to light the furnace. Unfortunately, the gas didn't seem to work. However, the water heater was an electric-type tankless unit, and we'd travel far enough south that snow hadn't covered the solar panels.

"Well, at least there's a fireplace upstairs. We should be able to light a fire so it can warm it up in here a little before attempting a shower or laundry," I said.

Gyrik grunted and followed me upstairs. When I moved toward the fireplace, he redirected me to sit on the sofa.

"Sit and stay warm. I'll start the fire and bring more wood inside," he said.

I watched him disappear outside after he started a small fire. Zach grinned at me as he set a tote on the table.

"You should decide if you like the princess role or not and tell him. He'll respect whatever your answer is."

"Princess role?"

"Yeah. My sister, Brenna, is…married, I guess, to one of them. Thallirin's a great guy. Patient. Kind. He was just a little too overprotective for Brenna's taste. She had to put her foot down to keep doing what she liked to do, which was archery. The fey are all a little like that when it comes to women. Overprotective. But they're not suppressive if you know what I mean. You just need to say when it's too much."

"Thanks for the advice," I said.

He nodded and left, and I turned to study the fire.

Was I imagining things, or had the back of Gyrik's black sweatpants looked wet?

CHAPTER TWELVE

GYRIK

WE'D LEFT THE CITY HOURS AGO, BUT I COULD STILL FEEL AVA'S warm breath on my chest. Each exhale had sent little shocks straight to my cock. It stirred at the memory but went dormant again as I listened to Zach suggest that Ava tell me she does not want to be treated like a princess.

Bram caught me frowning in the direction of the house.

"I take it Zach is running his mouth again," Bram said.

"Yes."

Zach emerged from the house and grinned and waved at me. It was a good thing Thallirin had patience.

"Do I need to talk to him?"

"No. He was trying to help her understand."

"Understand what?" Bram added another piece of firewood to the pile he was already holding.

"Why I lit the fire for her. That it was kind, but if she found it overbearing, she should tell me."

"Do you think she didn't like it?"

"She didn't seem angry when I left."

"Then he was probably just explaining things, trying to help smooth the way for you."

"Does it need to be smoothed?"

Bram stopped what he was doing to focus on me.

"Honestly, I don't know. Ava's different. She hasn't been living in fear for the past five months. She's been living in isolation. So, rather than jumping at every sound and trying to hide, she's... normal. Cautious but open. That works in your favor. Did she like talking to you?"

I thought back to the time we spent driving together.

"She seemed to enjoy talking to me."

She'd shared so many things about herself. Her favorite songs, which she sang for me, her favorite foods, clothes, weather, season, hairstyle—I knew so much about her. Yet, even after so much time together, I felt like I still barely knew anything.

"Well, women who choose to live alone and have cats are a different breed of women. They're more independent and have higher standards for who they allow into their lives. I'm not saying this to scare you, but...don't mess up. She might be a one-and-done chance."

"What does that mean?"

"It means this might be your only chance. If you screw up, she probably won't give you another chance."

The fear that she wouldn't want me as much as I wanted her grew until it became hard to breathe. What if I'd already said something wrong? What if she didn't like me lighting the fire for her? What if she didn't want to stay in Tolerance when we reached it? Or worse, what if she decided to like someone else?

The firewood in my arms fell to the ground.

"What is it? Infected?" Bram asked.

"No. I..." My gaze shifted to the house. "How will I know if I've messed up my chance already?"

Bram swore under his breath and called out. "Ava! I need you out here."

My panic increased.

"Don't look at me like that," Bram said quietly. "I'm helping."

Ava appeared at the door. Her gaze scanned the yard, landing on us.

"Gyrik just got really pale. Can you help him inside?"

She ran toward me, a look of concern on her face.

"I knew something was wrong," she said. "Come on. Let's get inside before you pass out. I don't think anyone here will be able to carry you."

She lifted one of my arms and fit herself against my side. The feel of her arm around my waist stopped my panic—and any other rational thought.

"See?" Bram said from where he still stood by the woodpile. "She's worried. Worry means she cares. If you'd messed up, she wouldn't care."

We were far enough away from Bram that I knew Ava hadn't heard him. Yet her arm tightened around my waist.

I glanced down at the top of Ava's head as she walked pressed up against my side. She looked up at me.

"Bram's right. You look pale. You shouldn't push yourself so hard."

She led me inside, walking past Zach and Will on the way to the bathroom. They watched us but didn't comment.

"Strip," she said, turning on the faucet.

I looked from her to the open door and back again.

"I need to see how bad it is," she said. "And I can't do that when you're wearing clothes."

She wanted to inspect me? What if she didn't like what she saw?

The panic, which had faded, flared again as I debated what to do. Should I undress, or should we talk about non-sex emotions first? Maybe I could make her one of the foods she liked. Or sing one of her songs to her. But I couldn't remember any of the words. No matter how hard I tried, nothing filled my head.

Her pretty blue eyes watched me expectantly.

"The water's warming. Hurry and shower. That last snow bath you took didn't get everything."

Slowly, I removed my shirt. Her gaze swept over my torso,

assessing and dismissive. I wanted to cringe and cover myself with the material again, but she motioned for me to turn around.

Reluctantly, I did. Her hands gripped the waistband of my sweatpants. My eyes went wide. The material was down around my ankles a second later.

I froze in full panic, hands slightly out to my sides.

A snort sounded from the doorway, and I turned to look at Zach, who was covering his mouth.

"It's not as bad as I thought," Ava said from behind me. "Zach, see if you can find some super glue. It'll burn, but it should hold it together until it heals. My grandpa used more than he should have and lived to tell the tales."

I didn't know what was happening and glanced at Zach.

"Your bite is bleeding," he said.

I twisted around to see myself in the mirror and spotted the twin half-moons carved into the top of my backside. I recalled bending to light the fire and feeling the pull back there when they'd reopened from the last stop but hadn't thought much of it. Bites healed quickly.

"Why didn't you say you were bitten?" Ava asked.

"I forgot."

I had. Just after it'd happened, my thoughts had been on washing quickly and rejoining Ava in the truck so she could keep telling me about her favorite sleeping position. After lighting the fire, I'd been more concerned with collecting wood for the fire so Ava would be warm enough.

"If someone had bitten my ass like that, nothing could have made me forget it," Ava said. "Now get in the shower and wash. With soap. I hope you're right about immunity and don't get any kind of infection once I glue that shut."

She left the bathroom, walking out past Zach, who was still grinning at me.

He glanced after her then leaned in to whisper, "If she looks mad, she's not. She's worried. Worried is good. It means she cares about you. Now, go shower."

I felt more reassured, hearing him say the same thing that Bram had, but still a little concerned about Ava's inspection.

Stepping under the water, I began to wash while trying to understand what had just happened. Ava had pulled down my pants to see all of me. She'd wanted to know how bad I was. She'd looked at me dismissively, but then she'd said I wasn't as bad as she thought.

Did that mean I was good?

I looked down at myself.

Angel said most women liked men with muscles. Some liked abs. Some liked pecs. Some liked forearms. She said preferences depended on the woman, just like males had preferences regarding females. Some liked breasts. Some liked butts. Some liked legs.

My brothers had asked why males didn't prefer a female's pussy. Angel said most men weren't attracted to a woman's pussy because it's not something they see all the time. Ghua said that was because human males didn't know how to talk their females into walking around without clothes.

The thought of Ava walking around with no clothes filled my mind, and I forgot what I was doing.

"Are you done?" Ava asked from the other side of the curtain.

I jumped a little, swallowed hard, and turned off the water.

"Yes."

When I opened the curtain, her gaze trailed slowly down my length, stopping at my hips. She didn't look angry or repulsed. Her expression softened slightly, and the corners of her mouth lifted an almost imperceivable amount.

Did looking at my cock make her happy?

I felt my cock stir under her direct attention. The tips of my ears heated.

"I…uh…sorry," she said, meeting my gaze. 'Here's a clean towel. I'll wait for you in the first bedroom once you're dry."

She pushed the towel at me, turned on her heel, and left.

I stared after her a moment before I hastily dried off and followed.

"Uh, Gyrik? You may want to use that towel you're holding to cover yourself," Will said. "Even if Ava's not intimidated by that, we are."

Zach howled with laughter as Bram chuckled. Ignoring all of them, I strode down the hallway and found the first bedroom door open. Ava was waiting inside, facing away from the door.

"Lie down on your stomach, please," she said, pointing to the bed.

I glanced at the towel I still held, disappointed that she hadn't looked at me again. Tossing it aside, I quickly lay on the clean sheets and turned my head to watch her let out a deep breath.

"Are you worried or angry?" I asked.

"I don't think I'm either. Maybe a little worried. Not at all angry."

I grunted, relieved she was still worried, as she approached the bed and sat beside me.

"The glue will sting, but Grandpa said it fades quickly enough. I'll need to hold the skin together for a few seconds while the glue dries. Ready?"

"Yes."

The first touch of her fingers against my bare skin almost drew a moan from me. Her hands were small and soft, cool against my warm skin. Her fingers danced over my backside below the bite. Teasing. Testing. Stroking.

A shiver ran through me. She noticed and mumbled an apology but didn't remove her hand.

She set it more firmly against my skin and started to knead the area like Mary kneaded her dough. I didn't shiver again as *want* rushed through me. The heat of my desperation for her melted me everywhere but surged aggressively in my cock. It hardened to the point of pain against the bed.

Closing my eyes, I fought not to groan as I imagined her hands moving from my backside to my front.

"Okay. I've got it right. Just a second. There. Don't move, or my fingers will be glued to your ass."

This time, a groan did escape me.

Don't let your desperation show.

How could I not, though? My desperation to hold her…to touch her…to kiss her was slowly consuming me.

"Sorry. I know it's not fun."

My cock bucked against the mattress when she blew on my skin.

"Better?"

I managed a jerky nod.

She released that section of skin and began gently pinching a little lower. A warning tingle began in my sack.

I was dying and didn't mind.

"One more," she said.

She held my skin and then blew on it.

I blinked, no longer seeing the room as the entirety of my existence shrank to where she held me and the growing tension between my legs.

"All done," she said, releasing me.

Denial ripped through me. We couldn't be done. Never.

I reacted to her abrupt abandonment and rolled over to grab her wrist and pull her toward me. It wasn't something I would have ever risked doing when thinking rationally. I only knew she couldn't leave me. I needed her.

She let out a little squeak as she fell onto my chest. Her pretty brown hair created a soft curtain around her face as she stared down at me.

Eyes wide, I blinked at her. Her body pressed against mine. I could feel the soft mounds of her breasts through her jacket, but more than that, I felt her *hand*.

A slow, soft smile curved her lips.

"You have no idea how lucky we both are."

I couldn't speak. Her palm covered my hard length, pressing it. Molding it. Cool. Soft.

Her hand was touching me.

The tingle spread to the base of my spine. My breathing increased, and I fought not to arch into her palm.

"If I hadn't dropped the glue, my hand would have been glued to this."

She *squeezed* me.

A small, choked sound escaped me before I arched and erupted.

CHAPTER THIRTEEN

AVA

Gyrik growled—a deep, resonating sound that should have been terrifying—as he came all over the place. It hit my jacket, my neck, my hair, his chest, his ear... It just kept spraying, and the only thing I could think to do was to slide my hand up his very impressive length to cap it with my fist and thumb.

His hand wrapped around mine, squeezing him tighter as he bucked into my hold. He kept going for another few seconds before stilling.

Stunned, I didn't move. I just stared down at him.

He was breathing heavily as his gaze, with pupils completely dilated, searched mine. His cheeks began to darken along with the tips of his ears.

"I'm sorry."

Those two simple words were filled with more sincerity and remorse than I'd ever heard in my life. And I'd heard it plenty of times.

Still studying me, he picked up the towel he'd tossed on the bed and wiped his release from my neck. Then he reached between us to dislodge my hand—I hadn't let go when he had—and wipe that clean, too.

My face ignited with heat. How could I have forgotten I was still holding *that*?

While I was distracted by some heavy self-recrimination, he stood with me in his arms.

"You'll need to wash your hair," he said, walking from the room.

Panic set in as he strode into the living room. The other three stopped what they were doing to stare at us.

Gyrik was naked. He had come on his ear and chest. *And he was carrying me.*

"Ah, do you need us to intervene, Ava?" Bram asked, his voice laced with uncertainty.

Shame kept my face red as I shook my head.

"If you need intervention, just scream," Zach said.

I wanted to hide, binge-eat some ice cream, and pretend none of this ever happened.

Thankfully, Gyrik was a fast walker and had us in the bathroom a few seconds later. He set me on my feet and tugged my jacket off before I knew what he intended.

"What are you doing?" I asked when he tossed it into the hallway.

"It needs to be washed."

I cringed, which was more distraction than I could afford because he took that opportunity to pull my shirt off. I clapped my arms around myself, not to save any modesty but because it was still cold on this side of the house.

"Uh, I'm okay getting undressed without help," I said when he reached for my jeans.

He pulled his hands back and watched me expectantly. So, I went with the more direct, but hopefully still kind, approach.

"You're probably cold and want to get dressed. I can shower by myself. You can go."

"I need your clothes to wash them."

Geez…how much had he come?

Rather than trying to look for it, I finished stripping out of my pants and handed them over. He proved he had only been waiting for that by walking out with them. I watched his glued-together backside disappear then stripped out of my bra and underwear without closing the door. The only heat source was in the living room, and I wasn't about to cut that off.

The water, which he'd showered in too, was barely body-temperature warm. I shivered through shampooing twice so I wouldn't have to repeat the experience.

Moving the curtain to the side, I almost screamed when I saw Gyrik standing there in a pair of shorts. He blinked at me then wrapped me in the towel he'd been holding.

"I heard you shivering," he said. "It's warmer by the fire. You should stay there until your hair is dry."

I nodded. He swept me into his arms and carried me out of the bathroom. Any protest died a fast death when I felt the heat radiating from him.

A blanket and a hairbrush waited by the fireplace in the living room. The other three weren't there, but I could hear them moving in the kitchen. Their presence was both reassuring and demoralizing. They'd witnessed what had to be the most awkward moment of my entire life.

Gyrik set me down on the blanket and wrapped it around me. I pulled it closer, appreciating the warmth.

I was a little surprised when I felt the first gentle tug on my hair.

He was brushing it.

"Tell me if I cause you pain," he said.

Too overwhelmed by the last twenty minutes, I nodded and let myself appreciate the quiet moment. Only the present mattered. Nothing happened before the hair brushing, and nothing would happen after. Well, I needed to get dressed after so I wouldn't freeze.

Thoughts of getting dressed led to thoughts of what had happened. I tried shutting those down but gave up after a while.

Sometimes, a girl just needed to overthink for a bit to sort out how she felt about something. And that was what I needed to understand. Was I okay with what had just happened, and did I still feel safe with Gyrik?

The way his fingers gently ran over my hair after each brush stroke was too soothing to feel anything but safe. And technically, what had happened in the bedroom wasn't his fault. Yes, he'd grabbed me to keep me from leaving, but I'd been the one to grab his cum-cannon, leading to the fateful misfire.

I shouldn't have squeezed it. But in all fairness, I'd still been in a state of denial even after the full-frontal view he'd given me in the bathroom. He couldn't have been that big. I had to have seen it wrong. A play of light, maybe.

But nope. He was every inch as big as I'd thought. And girthy too. No toy I'd ever owned could compete with him.

No, I didn't fear him. I was in awe. If anything, he should be the one afraid of me and my accosting hands. But he wasn't. And he wasn't making a big deal out of it. He'd apologized, helped me to the shower, washed my clothes, and was now brushing my hair.

So then, why was I feeling awkward?

Cum-cannon.

I just couldn't stop thinking about how much he'd shot everywhere. *I* was embarrassed but had no idea why. It wasn't like it was my cum. That was on him. Literally.

I giggled and hurriedly buried my face in the blanket. Then, I immediately felt guilty because I was laughing, and he was probably feeling a little embarrassed. No man wanted to pop off as fast as he had. At least, I didn't think they did.

That thought brought me around to what had caused it. I'd been gluing the bite on his butt shut. It couldn't have been very comfortable having me pinch something that was already looking a little bruised.

I froze.

Was he into hurt-kink?

I glanced back at him.

"Did I pull too hard?" His hand immediately went to the spot and started rubbing it gently. Everything he did with me was gentle. If he was into hurt-kink, it was only on the receiving end and not the giving. I could probably handle that.

Wait…what was I thinking?

"Ava?"

Realizing he was waiting for an answer to his question, I quickly said, "No, you didn't pull too hard. Not that I want you to pull harder."

God! Could I stop saying hard already?

"I think I'm having a har—difficulty processing what just happened. Are we okay?"

He blinked at me.

Confusion was the last thing either of us needed.

I glanced at the kitchen, where there were still indistinct sounds of conversation, then back to Gyrik.

"I'm sorry for landing on you like I did," I said quietly. "It wasn't intentional or planned or anything like that. I just want to make sure you're not feeling mad, embarrassed, or guilty…or anything like that."

"Are you?" Concern flitted across his expression.

"I'm not sure how I'm feeling. I think it'll depend on how you're feeling about what happened in the bedroom."

He swallowed visibly. "I liked it."

It was on the tip of my tongue to say, "Obviously," but I didn't. Instead, I tried to be honest as well.

"Yeah, I think I did, too, but not for the same reasons. The past few days have been so unreal. I think I'm still trying to process and accept everything on some level while not having a complete mental breakdown.

"What happened in the bedroom was a welcome distraction. Not that I want to repeat it. It's too cold for that. But I didn't hate it, and I'm not mad."

He studied me for a long moment then started brushing my hair again.

Taking the hint, I faced forward and closed my eyes. I let myself relax and enjoy it, which is what I'd wanted to do from the beginning. This time, though, it worked.

"Dinner's done when you guys are ready," Zach called from the kitchen.

Gyrik didn't stop brushing, so I said we'd join them in a few minutes and stayed where I was. The fire crackled, and its heat slowly warmed my face. Not inside the blanket, though. The damp towel wrapped around me felt like it wicked away any body heat I generated.

"Can you get my suitcase for me?" I asked Gyrik. "It's in the back of the truck."

Gyrik grunted, set the brush aside, and left.

I stood and let the blanket drop away. The heat from the fire sent a shiver through me as the dampness evaporated from my exposed arms and legs. But the air was still cold on my back. Especially my wet hair.

Gyrik returned a minute later with the suitcase, which he set down and opened for me.

I quickly pulled on some underwear under the towel and a T-shirt over the top. All the while, Gyrik watched me. But not in a creepy way. More like he was making sure I could do everything and didn't need help.

Once I was covered, I tossed the towel aside and tugged on some sweatpants, a sweatshirt, and socks.

"I don't know how you can walk around only wearing shorts when it's still cold in here."

He reached for the brush, but I stopped him.

"I'm going to grab some food first."

The only stops we'd made while driving were aftermath cleanups. While Gyrik washed in the snow, the rest of us went to the bathroom and refilled our bottles with the clean water from the back of Will's vehicle. So lunch had been a protein bar while driving, and I was hungry.

The conversation the other three were having at the table

stopped when we entered. I looked at the big pot of stew with noodles on the side then at the three men.

"Why do you all look guilty? Where are Pete and Repeat? That's not cat stew, is it?"

Zach snorted a laugh. "Your dark sense of humor is going to fit right in."

"Who said I was joking?"

Zach lifted Pete from his lap, and Bram held up Repeat. "We already fed them, but they're begging for more."

"Don't give in. If they get too fat, they might look more tempting." I took the bowl Will offered me. "Seriously, though, what was up with the expressions when we came in?"

All three looked at Gyrik. I did the same and saw his dark cheeks.

"Is there something you're not telling me?" I asked him.

"No, it's nothing like that," Will said, heaping my bowl with noodles and stew. "We're just worried that he's not respecting your boundaries."

It was the sweetest thing he could have said and helped put me at ease.

"I don't feel like any boundaries were intentionally crossed. But your concern means a lot to me. Thank you.

"If it's all right with all of you, I'm going to eat this by the fire so my hair can dry."

They nodded and waved me away.

Gyrik stayed behind.

CHAPTER FOURTEEN

GYRIK

In silence, we all watched Ava leave the kitchen. With guilt heavy in my heart, I faced the men who'd taken care of me as much as I'd cared for them. The disappointment in their gazes didn't surprise me. The entire time I'd brushed Ava's soft hair, I'd listened to their softly spoken reprimands.

"You're lucky she's still talking to you," Will said quietly once she was gone.

"I thought you were going to try to get to know her first and wait to put the moves on her until we were home," Bram said. "What happened?"

I rubbed the back of my neck and glanced at the doorway to the living room. I could hear Ava settling near the fire and wanted to join her, but I also needed advice.

"She was gluing the bite. It felt...good."

Zach snorted, and Will elbowed him.

"She stopped and was going to leave. I grabbed her hand. I didn't mean to. It just..." I sighed. "She fell on me. Her hand landed on my cock. It was warm and soft and—"

"We get the picture," Bram said.

"So it was a misfire?" Zach asked. "That's why it was all over?"

I nodded. "Ghua said that Eden gets very angry when it gets in her hair. That's why I carried her to the shower right away. Ava didn't seem angry, though. Do you think she liked it?"

Zach slammed his head down onto his arm on the table. The dishes rattled. His shoulders shook.

Uan and Thallirin were very patient males.

"I know it's tempting to toss him out the door," Bram said, seeming to hear my thoughts. "But remember how much Nancy loves him and how much Uan loves Nancy. Brenna and Thallirin too."

"Personally, I think Uan and Thallirin would understand a light tossing," Will said. "But back to the point. No, I don't think Ava actually *liked* it. I think she just understands it was an accident. If it happens a second time, I think she'll be a lot less forgiving."

I exhaled heavily, nodded, and took the bowl of stew Will offered me.

"It could have been worse," Bram said. "She's still talking to you, at least. Keep talking, and try not to bring up or even think about what happened. You don't want to scare her away."

With their warnings repeating in my mind, I went to join Ava. She looked up at my approach and smiled before glancing behind me.

"Don't they want to eat in here?"

I shook my head and sat down next to her.

"Do you think we'll reach one of your communities tomorrow?" she asked.

"Yes."

"Zach told me about them. Three big neighborhoods, each surrounded by a wall made out of cars. Enough room for everyone. A lot of the humans share homes, but the fey tend not to. Do you have your own house?"

"Not yet."

"Oh." I heard the disappointment in her voice.

"I gave my home to Etri and Fallor."

"That's nice of you, but where do you live?"

"I stay with them when I return, but mostly, I go out and look for survivors like some of my other brothers do, so I don't need a home yet."

"Zach said that, after I meet with June, Mya, and Andie, I'll be assigned a house. It's a little intimidating to think that I might be assigned a house to live in with strangers. Do you think Zach, Will, or Bram have room in their houses?"

I looked down at my stew to hide how much I didn't want her to want to live with anyone else but me.

"Gyrik?"

"Sorry, Ava," Zach said, entering the room and sitting heavily on the couch. "Our housing assignments have already been set. But don't worry. I have a feeling you're going to be assigned somewhere nice in Unity. It's the newest, and there are still plenty of open houses there."

"The one with the greenhouses and fields?"

"Yep. Your grandpa's seed books will be put to good use there. And if you hate gardening—"

"I don't," she said quickly.

"Then you should be fine. Want to play some more board games to pass the time?"

Relieved by the distraction, I joined them.

Human games were interesting. They didn't always make sense to me, but I liked playing and watching their excitement. They were as competitive with their paper games as my brothers and I were with our physical ones. Ava was no exception.

"Eat that and pay up!" she yelled, slapping her cards on the coffee table.

Zach, Will, and Bram grudgingly surrendered the candies they used to bet. The colorful little dots disappeared into Ava's mouth, and her happy little wiggle as she chewed captivated me. I reached across the table, stole three more candies from Zach, and slid them to her. She swiped them off the table, dodging his attempt to steal them back, and popped them into her mouth. She wiggled her shoulders from side to side.

"I'm calling it," Bram said.

"Yeah, I see how this is going to end. Gyrik is going to feed you all the M&M's," Zach said.

Ava grinned at me. "You can feed me chocolate any time."

I melted and tried to remember where Will had stored the chocolate we'd collected during this trip.

Will bumped into me. "Do you know that chocolate contains caffeine, and caffeine can keep people up at night?"

I blinked at Will. Zach shook his head at me, and I struggled to understand why.

"Are you hinting that I shouldn't have any more chocolate because I'll stay awake and not be ready at first light?" Ava asked. "This little bit of caffeine won't keep me up. The case of coffee beans I have in the back of the truck would, but I promise, I can still function on three hours of sleep. I've pulled all-nighters before where I pass out in my office chair, come to, make more coffee, and get back to work."

"That can't be good for you," Bram said.

Ava shrugged. "Sometimes sleep is overrated."

I thought of how she'd slept in my arms the night before and disagreed. Her sleep wasn't overrated. She needed it. Preferably while using me as a pillow again.

"I think you shouldn't have any more chocolate," I said.

"Finally," Bram said under his breath.

"Pfft. Sore losers," Ava said. "Let's play again tomorrow night. I have a fun-size pack of candy bars in one of those boxes."

"You're going to be popular back home," Zach said with a laugh that struck fear through me.

I didn't want Ava to be popular. I wanted her to be mine. But what did she want?

As they packed away the cards and set out their sleeping bags on the floor, I watched her move. She talked to everyone, making jokes and laughing prettily.

After she laid out her sleeping bag, feet toward the fire, she looked at me.

"I don't suppose you'd be willing to share with me again tonight, would you?"

I was on the sleeping bag faster than her eyes could track me. The way she slowly smiled sent a warning tingle to my shaft, and I quickly grabbed a spare blanket to pull over my waist.

She knelt down beside me, lifted my arm, and assumed the same position she had the night before, pressed against my side. This time, she reached behind her and tugged the arm she was resting on until I wrapped it around her waist. My cock twitched under the blanket, and I listened to the others settle in for the night.

I couldn't wait until we reached Tolerance.

"Is THAT IT?" Ava asked, leaning forward and pointing. She wasn't leaning forward to see but to stretch her back.

"It is. Would you like to pull over so I can drive?"

She laughed. "This close? No. I'm kind of nervous. You guys have been great, but we haven't seen any other people the entire time. Not counting the ones that were infected. What if your people don't want me here?"

"They will want you," I said, silently adding, "*I* want you."

She nodded and sat back, following closely behind Bram's supply truck.

As we neared, several of my brothers jumped over the wall.

"Damn," Ava said under her breath.

My gaze shifted from her to Dax and Bauts. Was she afraid of them, or did she like looking at them like she seemed to enjoy looking at me? Selfishly, I hoped it was fear.

She parked the truck, picked up Pete, and glanced at me.

"Well, I guess it's time to make new friends." She reached for the door, and I grabbed her shoulders to turn her toward me. Pete made a questioning sound from his place in her arms.

"You don't need to make more friends. I can be your friend."

Her gaze searched mine for several heartbeats.

"Is that what I am? Your friend?"

Don't be desperate. Don't be desperate.

"A friend for now, but maybe you would consider more once you get to know me better?"

Her slow smile made my pulse race.

"That's a good answer. Are you stopping me from getting out because you're worried I'll get to know someone else better first?"

"Yes."

"Okay. I promise to get to know you first. But I should still try to make other friends if I want to live here, right?"

I glanced at my brothers, who were watching us.

"Yes."

She considered me for a moment. "I'm nervous about fitting in here. I don't want to be alone like I was, but I don't want to live with strangers, either. Is there any chance I could live with you? I know you don't have a house, but what if there's room in my assigned house?"

I couldn't believe what I was hearing. "You want to live with me?"

"Yes."

I grinned widely. Her gaze shifted to my mouth, and her responding smile faded a little.

"There's still so much I have to learn," she said. "Your canines are really pointed. You don't bite like the infected, do you?"

"No," I said, no longer smiling.

Was she afraid of me now? Would she no longer want to live with me?

She nodded, reached around Pete to pat my arm, then eased from my hold to leave the truck.

"You carry Repeat," she said.

Unsure what her reaction meant, I hurried to lift up the soft animal and followed in her wake.

"You ready for a fun ride over the wall, Ava?" Zach called, getting out of the truck in front of us.

"You mean the same way they arrived?" she asked.

"Yep." Zach went to stand beside my brothers. "Ava, this is Bauts, and this is Dax. It might be easier if they carry the cats and Gyrik carries you."

"It's nice to meet you both. Are you all right with cats?"

"The better question is if the cats are okay with them," Will said, joining us.

Ava kissed the top of Pete's head and moved closer to Dax. My stomach twisted with the need to step between them.

"Dax, this is Pete. Would you mind holding out your hand so he can smell you?"

Dax did, and Pete immediately rubbed his face against Dax's knuckles. The animal had no sense of loyalty.

Smiling, Ava passed Pete to Dax and turned to me. "Repeat pretty much does whatever Pete does, but you should still let him smell Bauts."

Bauts reached out and scratched Repeat's head. "Animals like me."

Repeat's loyalty was just as bad as Pete's. Worse, actually. He crawled out of my arms to reach Bauts.

Ava laughed. "They're attention whores, aren't they? How do you want me, Gyrik?"

Logical thought ground to a halt as I thought of all the different ways I wanted Ava. First, just to hold her and touch her freely. Then, to kiss her…everywhere. Finally, to sink into her softness. Facing her. Lying on our sides. Behind her on my knees.

"Might not want to word it like that," Zach said.

Will elbowed him hard enough that the boy stumbled.

Dax reached out to steady him then went back to petting Pete while watching me stare at Ava. He knew what I was thinking.

"How do you want to carry me over that wall?" Ava clarified. "On your back?"

"No." I picked her up fast enough that she squealed and wrapped her arms around my neck the way I liked. "You can scream this time if you want."

Her eyes widened.

I ran at the wall and sprinted up it without warning her and listened to her sharp inhale as she clung to me.

CHAPTER FIFTEEN

AVA

THE GAG-WORTHY FEELING SETTLED AS GYRIK RUBBED MY BACK AND hugged me close. I could tell from the slant under my feet that we were on the top of the wall and not solid ground, but I hadn't lifted my head yet. Mostly, I was giving my stomach time to settle. But I also was giving my thoughts time to settle as well.

I was pretty sure Gyrik had just confessed to liking me before we got out of the truck. Why else would he say he wanted to be more than friends? I wasn't new at the dating game. I knew it could mean he wanted sex. And wanting sex wasn't synonymous with liking someone. But the way he'd been nervous about me making friends and how excited he'd been when I'd asked him to live with me suggested he wanted more from me than just sex.

My pulse, which had been settling, jumped again.

"I won't let you fall, Ava," Gyrik said against my hair. "Ever."

Comments like those were prodding me to give Gyrik a chance. As in a real chance, not just a one-night stand to satisfy my unrelenting curiosity about what sex with Gyrik would be like.

Probably mind-blowing.

"Ava?"

I even liked the way he said my name.

Lifting my head, I met his worried gaze. Whatever he saw when he looked at me seemed to reassure him, though, because he relaxed his hold just a little and nodded toward the homes stretched out before us.

The view was breathtaking from the top of the wall. It stretched as far as I could see. Nestled within the wall, the homes weren't lifeless or covered with snow as they'd been in Shakopee. Smoke curled from chimneys, and people walked around between the houses.

Actual people...moving around like life was *normal.* Yet, there were hints it wasn't. At least, not the version of normal I once knew.

"It's a lot bigger than I thought it would be," I said after studying it for several minutes. "Is that a cow in someone's yard?"

"Yes. We have a few cows here, but most of them are in Unity. Look there." He pointed toward a couple walking hand in hand down a street. The woman was human, and the guy was like Gyrik. "That is Mya and Drav. Would you like to talk to her about which home we can use?"

"Sure. Now is as good of a time as any."

Gyrik picked me up and stepped straight off the wall. My stomach somersaulted, and I barely suppressed my scream.

He landed in a jog that didn't stop until he reached the couple. The man looked a lot like Gyrik and like the other two had. All grey skin, pointy ears, and cat-like eyes, but long hair, unlike Gyrik. The eyes were a little different too. With the amount of green in his, they reminded me of something more reptilian, which was a little unsettling.

Realizing I was staring, I shifted my gaze to the woman's.

"Sorry. I'm still trying to process everything."

She smiled. "It does take some getting used to. But you look like you're doing all right."

Her gaze shifted briefly to Gyrik, and I looked up at him too, realizing I was still in his arms.

"Can you put me down, please?"

He did so but a little reluctantly. It was sweet, just like his panic in the truck had been.

I smiled at him then turned to the woman whose permission we needed to live together.

Holding out my hand to her, I said, "My name's Ava, a recently discovered survivor who accepted Gyrik's invitation to check out your community. You're Mya, right?"

"I am." She shook my hand. "And I'm glad you're here. Are there more in your group?"

"She was living alone," Gyrik said.

"Alone?"

"Alone and oblivious, apparently," I said. "I only discovered what had happened a few days ago."

"What? How? No, wait. I think this conversation needs to wait until we're inside. It's still not warm enough for me out here."

She gestured toward a side street, and we started walking.

"You wouldn't have liked where Gyrik found me, then," I said. "It snowed the day we left. He had to run in front of the trucks so we knew where to drive."

"I'm glad we didn't get that much snow." She glanced behind us. "Are those your cats?"

I looked back and saw Bauts and Dax surrounded by other fey who were petting my boys.

"They are."

"Good. We need more animals around here. They're not fixed, are they?"

"Pete is. Repeat isn't. He was too young before all this happened."

"That's great! We have a girl cat here who needs a boy cat."

She turned up the sidewalk to one of the many houses and opened the door. No lock. Just an opened door.

"So, my cats get to stay? Does that mean I can too?"

She laughed as the big grey man behind her helped her out of her jacket inside. Her baby bump was noticeable enough that I did a double-take.

"Just about five months now. It's hard to tell how much time has passed. We haven't been great at tracking the days."

I glanced from her to the big man beside her.

"Yes, he's the father," she said. "And I'm not the only one."

A little of the shock and concern I felt must have shown because she quickly held up her hands.

"No, no. I don't mean that he's fathered a lot of kids. I mean, I'm not the only woman pregnant with a fey baby. There are a few other women like me. I'm the furthest along, though."

My relief that I hadn't joined some kind of harem was palpable.

"Oh. Congratulations then."

She laughed and motioned to the couch.

"And I think you're going to fit in well whichever community you choose."

"I get to choose?" I asked, sitting beside her. "I thought housing was assigned."

"Eh, only for the people who we think won't make the right choices for themselves or might cause trouble."

"How do you know I won't cause trouble?"

"Because you're with Gyrik. Not just *with* him but treating him like a person."

I glanced at Gyrik, feeling sad again as I recalled the mistreatment Zach had told me about.

"Now tell me your story," Mya said. "How did you not know what happened?"

We sat in the living room, and I retold everything from saying goodbye to my family to shutting myself off from the world so I could finish my project to discovering Silver Bay to Gyrik showing up during my final bathroom run.

"How did you not panic? When I first saw Drav, I was close to having a heart attack."

"I think I was just so happy to know I wasn't alone that I

hugged first. It helped that it was dark out and I couldn't see him clearly. It was a little bit of a shock when he walked into the cabin, though. The underlying panic was there but more because his differences proved what he was saying was true."

"So you were panicking more about the end of the world than the fact you were meeting a fey face to face."

"Pretty much." I reached into my pocket and pulled out the picture of my family, which Gyrik had thankfully not washed. "Any chance these faces look familiar to you? It's my mom, grandpa, and sister."

She looked at the picture—really looked—and then shook her head. "I'm sorry. They aren't. But we can pass that picture around. Actually…" She trailed off, lost in thought for a moment. "That's a really good idea."

"What is?" I asked.

She focused on me again. "I'm not sure how much Gyrik's told you; groups like his are searching for more of us.

"Your reaction to Gyrik was an exception to what they've come to expect. Humans greet them with fear and hostility. So far, you're the first one the groups have found who has accepted their invitation. Maybe if we had pictures of all the survivors who are here, waiting for their loved ones, more might be willing to join, or we might actually reunite people."

"I'll admit that I was a little worried about leaving with Gyrik and his group. Not because I was worried about Gyrik specifically but because four strangers were promising me a safe haven after telling me the world had ended. It sounded a little too good to be true."

"And when something sounds too good to be true, it probably is," she said in understanding. "Would pictures have helped?"

"I don't know. They would have if I'd seen my family in them, but if not, I probably would have still hesitated. I guess it depends on the types of pictures that were taken."

She looked at Drav. "This should go both ways. Not just pictures of people here but people they're looking for too. We should talk to Brooke and see if she's willing to make sketches of missing family members. The next supply group that goes out should watch for instant print cameras so we can take pictures of the people we find out there too."

I watched Drav stride toward the door and glanced at Gyrik, unsure what to do. Was that a hint we should leave?

Before I could ask, Mya said, "You're welcome to stay for lunch and meet more of the residents here in the Tolerance community. Or if you'd rather have Gyrik take you for a tour, that's fine too."

"I'll take Ava," Gyrik said, setting his hand on my shoulder.

Mya grinned. "I was hoping you'd say that."

Because she wanted me out? Still unsure, I stood.

"If you're looking for open houses here, there are a few on the west side. Personally, I'd avoid looking for a place in Tenacity. It's overcrowded, and although June and Matt cleaned out the really bad apples, it's still a tense environment over there. If you want a place that's more harmonious with the fey, stick to here or Unity, our newest community. They have a lot of unclaimed homes there."

"That's the one with the greenhouses and fields, right?" I asked.

"It is. Are you interested in being a farmer?"

"My grandpa was really into gardening. I have a few binders filled with the seeds he collected over the years. He made notes about hardiness and yield. He was really into it and liked to talk about it. I wouldn't mind trying to put some of that information into practice. No guarantee I'd be any good at it, though."

"You won't know until you try. And this is the perfect time for it. I suggest heading there first."

I nodded, stood, and held out my hand. "It was nice to meet you, Mya."

"You too. Thanks for accepting Gyrik's invitation. I hope you two find a house you like in Unity."

Gyrik took my hand and led me to the door where Drav spoke

to another fey. I smiled politely at both of them as they stepped aside, allowing us to leave.

Once we were a good distance away, I looked at Gyrik.

"I can't tell if that meeting went well or not. Were we just kicked out?"

He blinked at me.

Where was Zach when I needed him?

"Nevermind. What do you think of Mya's idea of checking out Unity to find a house? You're still willing to live with me, right?"

The idea of snuggling with Gyrik every night appealed to me...a lot. And if a few more impromptu explosions happened because of it, my ego wouldn't mind the boost. He was easy to talk to and easy to be around. His teeth had surprised me a little, but he really did have a heart-melting smile when he let it free.

And most importantly, I felt really, really safe with him around. And appreciated. And cared for.

I realized I'd already started the slow fall, which hadn't been very slow. I really *liked* Gyrik.

As I waited for an answer, the tips of his ears darkened. I needed to ask Zach what that meant.

"Yes, I want to live with you, Ava," he said finally.

My smile was so wide it strained my cheeks.

"Perfect. Let's find Pete and Repeat and head over there. You know how to get there, right?"

"I do."

As we walked back toward the wall, I noticed how many people were walking around and how many of them weren't human. Men just like Gyrik wandered between the houses. I saw one walking a cow on a leash.

"Well, that's something new," I said. He made eye contact with me, and I waved.

Gyrik caught my hand, and I fought not to grin.

"Pete and Repeat are there," he said, pointing down the road.

My two cats were twining around the legs of a group of

gathered fey. One would occasionally squat down to give a cat a pet and stand again when the cat walked away.

Still holding my hand, Gyrik led me toward them.

Pete saw me drawing near and abandoned the group to stroll my way. Gyrik released my hand so I could scoop Pete up and give him the smooches he enjoyed.

"We are going to Unity and will need an escort," Gyrik said while I rained my love onto Pete.

Several of the fey stepped forward. Gyrik nodded and took Pete from me to pass off to one volunteer. Then I was in Gyrik's arms again, fighting against the urge to gag as he jumped over the wall.

At the top, he paused, which gave my stomach a moment to settle while the others jumped down by the trucks. Bram and Zach, who were still unloading with some other fey, called out greetings, and I watched how they interacted. The way the fey responded was more reserved but still familiar and friendly.

"Are you ready?" Gyrik asked.

"I am. Thank you."

His arms tightened around me, pressing me firmly against his chest, which helped me feel a little more secure when he stepped off the edge. After he landed, he smoothed his hand down my back as I clung to him.

"Thank you," I mumbled into his chest, not yet ready to let him go.

CHAPTER SIXTEEN

GYRIK

I HELD AVA AND WAITED FOR HER PULSE TO CALM FROM THE JUMP down. She felt so good in my arms. But the way she wrapped her arms around my waist and held me in return was even better.

My brothers glanced at us and grinned knowingly.

I'd found my female, and I would never let her go. However, when she lifted her head and looked up at me, I knew I needed to. Temporarily. I brushed the hair back from her face that had come loose, and she smiled as she released me.

"What do you think?" Zach asked, walking over to us. "Are you staying?"

"Mya said that I could choose which community," Ava said. "Gyrik and I are going to tour Unity. Since my day job no longer exists, I'll need something to occupy my time, or I'll go crazy. Gardening seems like a good fit."

One of my brothers near Bram asked him, "Why is sex not an occupation?"

Bram choked on his laughter as they waited for his answer. Ava glanced at him, but I knew she hadn't heard the question. They were too far away and spoke softly. It was a good question, though, and I was about to ask Ava when she looked up at me.

"You have a lot of experience gardening, right? You said there were fields in the caves that you tended?"

I nodded.

"Good. Then we can be farmers together."

Together. The way she said it warmed my chest.

"Well, all your supplies are still in your truck except for the generator and the batteries," Zach said. "If you don't mind, we'll allocate those to wherever they're needed most."

"That makes sense." Her gaze found mine again. "Are you ready?"

Ready to live with her? Ready to hold her in my arms every night? I nodded as my heart beat faster in anticipation.

"If Unity isn't a good fit, come back here. I know you'd like living in Tolerance," Zach said.

"I'll keep that in mind," Ava said as she moved toward her truck.

Bauts opened the passenger door for her and handed her Pete. I took Repeat from Ashkii and got in.

"Are they going to take that truck?" Ava asked, nodding toward the one Bram and my brothers were almost done unloading.

"No. They will run." I started the engine and set Repeat on my shoulder so he could make himself comfortable. He jumped to the headrest, using it and my neck to lie down.

"How far away is Unity?" Ava asked, watching my brothers as I turned the truck around.

"Not far."

I started down the road, and they kept pace. She sat back in her seat and sighed, petting Pete. When I glanced at her, she was staring straight ahead, wearing a small frown.

"Are you angry?" I asked.

"No, I'm wondering what life will be like now. It's kind of annoying thinking of how much time I spent learning something that doesn't even exist anymore. I think that's why I like the idea of Unity and gardening. No matter what, growing food won't be a waste of time." She looked down at Pete and played with his ear.

Heat flooded my shaft at the thought of her touching my ear like that.

She sighed again. "I'm a logic-based person. Logic says I probably won't ever see my family again, and I guess I'm feeling a little lost."

I reached across the seat and threaded my fingers through hers.

"There might not be as many humans as there were, but there are still survivors out there. If your sister is as smart as you are, you will see her again."

The corner of Ava's mouth curved. "Smart? I was just plain lucky. The world has changed so much, Gyrik. I really hope they survived it."

I rubbed my thumb over her soft skin. "The world has changed, but not all of the changes are bad."

"Tell me the good ones so I can focus on those."

"Cleaner air. When we first arrived, the air tasted bad. It's different now. Better. Humans now have the freedom to do what they want. Ryan told us how the world was. You needed to work, not to survive but to please others. Slaves to those who had more money and power."

"Eh, I'm not sure that's how I would view that, but I understand what you're trying to say. Not all changes are bad. The air *is* cleaner. And it's quieter. Soothing."

Her fingers traced over mine before she pulled away and looked out the window again.

Unity's main gate opened as we approached. Ryan waited inside near the space he'd made for the supply trucks to park.

"That's Ryan?" Ava asked as I stopped the truck. "He's a lot younger than I'd imagined him."

I glanced from her to him. She was studying him closely. Why? Did Ava think Ryan was handsome?

Looking at Mya's brother, a man who was always willing to help and support us, I wondered if he would be opposed to living in a different community for a while.

He grinned at me and waved as I passed Repeat to Ava and got out to hurry around the truck to open the door for her. I passed the cats to my brothers and took her hand to help her down.

"Hey, Gyrik. Mya radioed you'd be joining us with a new friend."

Ava smiled and held out her hand to Ryan. "I'm Ava."

I took her hand in mine and brought it to my side. She looked at me with surprise, but that faded as she smiled, and a pretty pink flushed her cheeks.

She glanced at Ryan. "Sorry."

"Don't worry about it. I'm used to it. I heard you brought some very welcome pets."

"Yeah, I'm pretty sure Repeat's engaged."

Ryan laughed and nodded while my fingers traced over Ava's. Would she give me a ring to claim me as hers like Brooke claimed Solin?

"Allow me to give you a tour." Ryan motioned to the street, and I listened to Ryan tell Ava about Unity as we walked with him.

"My sister mentioned you recently learned what's been happening these last few months. It must be a bit of a shock."

"Yeah. It's going to take some getting used to."

"I bet. Honestly, the worst part is going to be that you can't run to the corner store for milk and eggs when you run out. But that's what we're hoping to make Unity into, maybe not the corner grocery store but the place you can go to for some of the things you used to find at one. Produce first. Eventually more, like milk and eggs."

"I saw the cow in Tolerance. Gyrik mentioned you have some here, too. I didn't know about the chickens, though."

"We don't have a lot of them yet. I found an incubator, and one of the fey found a rooster, but it'll take time to increase the flock and the production. Time and the right people."

My stomach tightened as I looked at Ryan. Was he saying Ava wasn't the right person?

"We're not looking to rebuild things the way they were," he continued. "We want people who want to be a part of building a better, safer future. People who aren't focused on getting more than their neighbor, you know?

"Our goal is to have our communities run on a fair-trade system. Maybe we grow the produce, Tenacity bakes the bread, and Tolerance makes the clothes. Who knows? We're not worried about getting anything out of it but surviving collectively."

Ava nodded but said nothing.

"It's a lot to take in, I know. But I want you to know I'm interested in hearing your thoughts, whatever they might be, when you're ready to share them. We can't make a community thrive unless all the voices are heard. That doesn't mean everyone will get their way. It means listening, compromising, and pitching in to be a part of something. If that sounds good to you, the unoccupied houses have the flag up on the mailbox."

"That's it? Just pick a house and move in."

"Yep. That's it. We've made sure they all have a heat source. We fitted them with outdoor wood furnaces or wood stoves if they didn't already have a fireplace. Not all of them have solar yet, but we have generators we can move if you like one without solar."

"Why bother with electricity? Gyrik said the light draws in the infected."

Gyrik said…

Gyrik said…

My cock twitched. I wanted to pull Ava into my arms and

breathe in her scent. More than that, I wanted to kiss her and taste her until my name was the only thing she could say.

"And even if the walls keep them out," she continued, oblivious to the direction of my thoughts, "eventually, the solar panels will fail like all the appliances. Wouldn't it be better to start out less dependent on what we once had?"

Ryan shrugged. "Adapting takes time. We've lost so much already. Small comforts now might make it easier to lose the rest more slowly."

I thought back to my conversation with Ava. Humans truly had lost so much while my brothers and I had gained everything. Guilt flooded me, and I silently vowed that I would do everything I could to help her live a comfortable life.

She glanced back at me. "Do you like any of these houses?"

"I like any house you like," I said.

She smiled and looked at Ryan. "Do you mind if we walk through some of them?"

"Help yourselves. I better get back to the fields. We have a lot to clear so we can plant."

He dipped his head in farewell and jogged away. Ava stared after him. My worry grew.

"I feel guilty that I'm so far behind everyone else. Ryan already seems fine. Adjusted. How old is he?"

"He's still a child."

"No. He's eighteen," Bauts said, correcting me. "Mom told me."

I wanted to growl at Bauts.

"Mom?" Ava asked.

"Mya and Ryan's mom," Bauts said. "But she said she will be our mom, too, since we don't have one."

Ava looked from Bauts to me, her expression hard for me to read.

After a moment, she said, "Well, let's see if Pete and Repeat like any of these houses."

Ava and her cats decided on a one-story home at the end of a block near the back of the community. She liked the house because it had a large backyard and because one of the cars in the nearby section of wall reminded her of her grandfather's.

Bauts and Ashkii helped carry the supplies from the truck and left afterward.

I watched Ava set up the cats' litterbox in the corner of the second bathroom and their food and water bowls in the kitchen. The way she moved and her quiet words to the animals created a sense of peace that I'd never known before. I could watch her endlessly and never tire of it.

"Now what?" she asked, not looking at me.

Images of hugging and kissing Ava for hours flashed through my head, but I knew it was too soon for that. I didn't just want Ava's body—although I did want that, too…very badly—I needed to win her heart and mind so she would stay forever.

"Are you hungry?" I asked instead. "We could make a meal together."

"Sure. What are you hungry for? I have cans of tuna, chicken, and some jerky. Not sure what we can do with that other than eat it. Honestly, that's what I normally do. I tend not to spend a lot of time making meals. Mostly because I didn't have the time, not because I didn't like it."

As she talked, she moved around the kitchen, putting items into cabinets.

When she climbed onto the counter to reach the top shelf for some supplies, I quickly moved behind her, worried she'd fall. She turned to hop down and saw me standing there at the same time.

Her eyes widened, and her hands caught on my shoulders as she tipped forward.

I grabbed her waist as her mouth bumped against mine. Soft. Warm. Inviting.

CHAPTER SEVENTEEN

AVA

I froze with my mouth pressed against Gyrik's firm lips.

His hands twitched on my sides where he lightly gripped me, likely to catch my fall. Jerking back, I looked at Gyrik and opened my mouth to apologize.

Words died as his gaze dropped to my lips, and I watched his pupils expand so much that his irises almost disappeared.

My pulse skipped.

I glanced at his mouth.

When I looked up again, he was watching me with an intensity that should have made me nervous. Instead, it goaded me.

"Can I kiss you, Gyrik?"

His fingers twitched on my sides again.

"Yes."

Leaning in, I brushed my lips against his a second time, testing the texture and feel of his mouth without going any further than a lip nibble. It'd been so long since I'd kissed someone. I'd forgotten how amazing it was. Or maybe it was just Gyrik.

When I pulled back, he blinked at me. Was he confused about how to kiss, or did he not like kissing me?

"Should I kiss you again?" I asked.

"Yes."

The subtle growl behind that word made my knees weak, and I eagerly leaned in for another kiss. This time, I licked his bottom lip before sucking it into my mouth, and he gave a very definitive reaction.

He spun us around and lay me on the island counter. One hand gripping my side and the other cradling the back of my head to cushion it, he stared down at me for half a heartbeat before his mouth covered mine. I braced for aggression, but what I got was tender, featherlight brushes of his lips against mine, trailing to the side and along my jaw. When he reached my neck, I felt his tongue—the barest of touches—as he nibbled and tasted my skin.

I relaxed into the sensation of his mouth against my skin.

The hand on my side flexed, lightly kneading me before gliding down to my waist and dipping under my shirt to touch my bare skin. It wasn't anything indecent, but it ignited a need I hadn't felt in a long time.

Wrapping my arms around his shoulders, I threaded my fingers in his hair and turned my head to kiss his temple.

A knock on our front door startled me from my daze, and I pushed against Gyrik's chest. He immediately released me so I could scramble off the counter and hurry to answer the door.

The woman standing there smiled widely at me. She was a little older than me, maybe close to thirty, with shoulder-length medium-brown hair thrown into a low ponytail and warm brown eyes that were as welcoming as her smile.

"Hi, neighbor! I'm in the house across the street. I'm not interrupting anything, am I?"

"No," I said, hoping my clothes were straight.

"Oops. I guess I did interrupt something," she said, looking behind me.

I glanced back, and my mouth dropped open at the sight of Gyrik standing there with the most massive boner tenting his pants that I'd ever seen in my life. It was so big it looked fake, but I knew it wasn't. I'd seen what he was packing. Touched it, too.

Snapping my mouth shut, I faced the woman.

My expression had to be comical because she laughed and waved away my worry.

"It happens more than you think," she said. "My name's Allison. I live with Courtney, Kennedy, and Hanno. Since you're new here, I thought I'd come over and introduce myself."

"Come in. Please."

"Are you sure?" Her gaze once again went to the front of Gyrik's pants.

"I'm sure."

She grinned at me as I stepped back.

"Did you two just get together?" she asked.

I glanced at Gyrik, not sure what to say. He met my gaze, saying nothing but with no judgment in his gaze despite the unflagging tent he still sported.

"I'm going to take that as a yes," Allison said, drawing my attention.

I quickly shut the door. "Sorry. I'm still new to all of this."

"Hey, I get it. I'm new to it myself. Same with Courtney and Kennedy. They're with Hanno now."

I led her toward the living room as I tried to decipher what she was saying. Then I decided to just be bluntly nosey. I needed to understand what I was getting into.

"Are all three of you with him?" I asked hesitantly as I sat on the couch. She didn't look at all offended by the question as she joined me.

"No. I'm with Hanno. Courtney and Kennedy are with each other and respectfully using Hanno to gain immunity and possibly get pregnant. They wanted a baby together before all of this happened, and that hasn't changed. Just the method has.

"I know it sounds weird, but it's actually kind of nice not being the only one responsible for his sex drive. Sex with someone as big as they are isn't always fun. For me, it hurts afterward.

Sometimes for days. He's super sweet, though. He feels bad every time and always tries to be so gentle. And when it hurts, he doesn't want me to do any of the chores. Just rest.

"But for both our sakes, I'm grateful Courtney and Kennedy are there. Even though they aren't into men, they help out whenever I need a break. At first, he was really insecure about me loaning him out until he understood that they love each other and not him."

I sat back, trying to process what she just openly unloaded.

She grinned at me. "Yeah, I never thought I'd be in this kind of relationship either. There's a woman in Tenacity who is with two fey. I couldn't imagine trying to keep up with two of them. I'd never be able to walk again. But I hear she's really happy and very pampered."

I glanced at Gyrik, who was watching me closely as he sat in a chair opposite me. Was the focus because of the boner or because he knew I was now questioning his motive for bringing me here?

Facing Allison, I asked, "What did you mean by immunity? The fey can make us immune?"

Her humor faded to shock. "You're new-new, aren't you?"

"Yeah. Gyrik and his group found me a few days ago in northern Minnesota."

"You seriously need to come over after sunset and tell us about that. I'd ask now, but I know Courtney and Kennedy will want to hear about it firsthand, too. We don't get too many new people.

"But to answer your question, yes, the fey can make us immune. The scientists are just wrapping up their research. Sex is the key. Something about the fey, uh, 'fluids' being absorbed by us. The most effective way is intercourse. Oral works, too, but it's slower and a lot to swallow. If you have TMJ, I really wouldn't recommend that route."

I looked down at my hands. I'd asked Gyrik if they were looking for a woman, and he hadn't answered.

"Just women or men too?"

"Well, I haven't heard of any fey interested in sleeping with men yet," she said, misunderstanding my question. "But a few of the fey donated fresh samples, if you know what I mean, for oral shots. Not many men volunteered to take them, though. If I were a man and needed to drink another guy's semen for immunity, I'd be the first in line, no hesitation. Not all of them can get over the stigma, though." She shrugged lightly.

"So I wasn't just brought back here for sex?" I asked.

Allison's eyes went wide. "What? No. Don't get me wrong... the fey *are* interested in finding women. But if you'd been a guy willing to join our community, you would have been welcomed, too. Maybe not with as much enthusiasm, though." She looked pointedly at Gyrik's crotch, which was still tented.

When her gaze met mine again, it held compassion. "I'd love to stay longer, but I told Hanno I'd only be gone for a few minutes. He gets nervous that I'll leave him when he's with them. He'll let them take their time if I stay in the house."

She stood.

"Them?" I asked before I could stop myself.

She grinned. "Yeah, Courtney says they take turns on his face and his pole while making out on top of him. It pretty much makes it seem like the poor guy isn't there even when he's busting a nut for them."

I think my mouth fell open again because she paused on the way to the door and held up her hands. "Don't get me wrong. They don't mistreat him, and his favorite food is tuna tacos. Mine, obviously, but he doesn't seem to mind theirs either."

"Um. Okay. I promise I didn't even think about him being mistreated."

I was pretty sure having two girls make out on top of a guy was most guys' fantasy, but I didn't say that.

At the door, she held my hands in hers. "They're really nice, and I hope I didn't shade your opinion of them. Like I said, they're a godsend for me. I appreciate that they're interested enough in immunity to help me. They feel like sisters. We all take care of each other."

It made me think of how my sister would have reacted to sharing a man with me. She would have been revolted, and that made me want to laugh. At the same time, my heart ached with missing her.

"I like the sound of having sisters, honestly."

Allison smiled gratefully before opening the door and motioning to the yellow house across the street. "Feel free to come on over if you need anything, like a friendly ear or just a timeout. There's almost always someone home. And if you're bored after dark, we usually play cards. You're welcome to join us any night. Good luck."

"Thanks."

I'd barely closed the door when arms wrapped around me from behind.

"Please don't share me, Ava."

For a moment, I was confused, but then I realized Gyrik had misinterpreted my comment about liking Allison's situation. He thought I wanted the same setup. I didn't. I just liked the sound of having someone to depend on. However, his insecurity soothed away the concerns that had surfaced during my conversation with Allison about what Gyrik might want.

Leaning my head back against him, I patted his arms. "I won't."

He spun me around, and his gaze searched mine. The worry I still saw there softened me more.

"What are you looking for?" I asked gently.

"Fear."

I shook my head. "What are you worried I'm afraid of?"

"Me."

"I'm not."

"Sex with me."

"Actually, even though I'm a little intimidated after that conversation, I'm also even more curious and a little excited. I've seen and touched what you're working with."

His pupils went wide again.

"Are you still hungry?" he asked.

"Not for food. I think I'd like to pick up where we left off."

I stood on my toes, wrapped my arms around his shoulders, and kissed him to ensure he understood.

He groaned and picked me up, gripping my legs as he wrapped them around his waist. The hint of aggression spiked my libido, and I deepened the kiss. I thought he was going to drop me at the first touch of my tongue against his and squeaked into his mouth as he stumbled a step. His hold tightened, and my back pressed against the wall a second later.

Any hint of hesitation on his part vanished. He kissed me hungrily, devouring my mouth in a way that I'd never experienced yet absolutely loved. When he broke away to kiss and nibble my neck, I clung to his shoulders and let him have his way.

The wall behind me vanished. Before I could question it, his hand slid further under my thigh, and his fingers stroked my center over my jeans.

Need shot straight through me. Need to get undressed. Need to kiss him more. Touch him.

I was panting with need.

How long had it been since I'd had sex?

Too long. Way too long.

I needed him now.

My back hit a mattress, and his mouth left my neck. He leaned back and searched my gaze.

"What are you looking for?" I asked.

"Permission."

How could one simple word make me want to rock his world so badly?

"Get naked, Gyrik," I said, pushing him off of me enough to tug at my shirt.

He blinked at me as he pulled my shirt off, and I paused, breathing hard and questioning whether I'd read the situation wrong.

"Sex. Yes or no?"

"Yes."

"Then move so I can get naked too."

He had my pants and underwear off before I even felt his hands on me.

Then he paused again, staring *there*.

I'd shaved a few days ago, so I knew it wasn't a complete jungle, but the way he stared unblinkingly at it made me a little self-conscious.

"Uh, I think I'll take a shower first," I said.

I rolled off the bed and made it two steps before he picked me up from behind.

"I'll help you," he said against my neck, once more kissing me there.

CHAPTER EIGHTEEN

GYRIK

AVA TILTED HER HEAD, GIVING ME MORE ACCESS TO HER NECK. IT gave me hope that she hadn't changed her mind.

I knew I'd upset her enough that she'd wanted to run, but I didn't know how. It was too late for running, though. She'd asked me to live with her...asked if she could kiss me.

Get naked, Gyrik.

Sex. Yes or no?

When we reached the bathroom, I stopped in front of the mirror and lifted my head to look at her. She was perfect. Soft. Rounded in all the right places.

"It makes me uncomfortable when you stare at me like that," she said, meeting my gaze. "Can you put me down?"

My arm tightened around her, and I kissed her neck again.

"Do you want me to release you because you don't like being held or because you're afraid?"

"Neither. I'm embarrassed and want to cover up."

I groaned against her skin, understanding the problem. Humans loved to cover themselves.

"You're the first female I've seen without clothes." Using my free hand, I lightly ran my fingers over her shoulder and down her side. "Everything about you fascinates me. I want to touch and kiss you everywhere. I want to learn what you like and what you don't like. But I can't do that if you run from me and cover yourself."

I palmed her breast and tested the sensitivity of her nipple. Her lips parted, and her gaze became unfocused when I gently plucked at it.

She shivered in my arms.

"Are you cold?"

"No."

I dipped my head to her neck to test her responses there. I knew she liked my kisses, but I found she liked my teeth even better. She relaxed in my hold as I explored her for a few more moments.

"Do you still want me to put you down?" I asked.

"No." Her hands clutched my forearm under her breasts as her head fell back to my shoulder, as I carefully left a red mark on her skin.

"Mmm. My brave Ava," I said, kissing the indent between her shoulder and neck.

A soft whimper escaped her. I used my teeth. She whimpered louder, and her legs twitched.

"Sex. Yes or no?" I asked, repeating her words.

"Yes," she breathed.

I released her nipple, which I'd been toying with, and turned on the shower. While the water warmed, I focused on the other side of her neck and skimmed my free hand over her belly.

She tensed even as her lips parted with a sigh.

"If you tell me to stop, I will," I said, even as I doubted myself.

I needed a taste of her, no matter how small.

My mouth watered, and I glanced up to watch my hand in the mirror. That tuft of brown hair between her legs mesmerized me. For so long, I'd yearned to see a pussy for myself, and now that I had, I couldn't look away. Hidden by soft curly hair and with a scent that begged for my tongue, it was as beautiful as my brothers had claimed.

If she hadn't panicked, I would have already been feasting.

Moving slowly and distracting her with small bites on her tender neck and shoulder, I moved my hand to that hidden valley. When I reached it, I used my fingers to part it for my view. My cock bucked at the glistening sight.

I ran my fingertip over the little bump my brothers promised would bring a female great pleasure. Ava's unsupported legs twitched against mine as she whimpered and moved her hips, pressing into my touch.

"Shower," she rasped.

I turned toward the water, tested it, and decided it was warm enough. The second I had us in the shower, I spun her around and dropped to my knees in front of her. Her hands grabbed my shoulders, and she widened her stance to steady herself.

"What are you—"

Her words died abruptly as I dove for the taste I needed. It was slightly sweet, a little salty, and absolutely addicting. I lapped at her pretty little pussy from bottom to top, long strokes of my tongue that didn't miss a drop of her essence.

"Oh my God," she said, gripping my shoulders tighter.

My cock wept at the sound of her voice, and the telltale warning at the base of my spine grew as she repeated the words several times.

I knew from my brothers it was a good phrase that meant she was praising my skill at tasting her. When she said it twelve times —a number Ghua promised was perfect—I used my tongue to explore her opening. It squeezed me as I pressed my tongue upward, using firm pressure to lick there.

Ava's fingers tangled in my hair, and her knees bent as the channel around my tongue began to quiver. My cock throbbed. Her keening cry echoed in the tiled space. It was the most beautiful sound. As beautiful as the pussy trying to suck my tongue.

With a grunt, I released into the bottom of the shower.

Before her pussy pulses stopped, I replaced my tongue with

my fingers. Merdon swore during a female's release was the perfect time to trick a smaller pussy into accepting more than it thought it could. And Ava's pussy felt very small. Thankfully, two of my fingers slipped in easily. Her opening fought the addition of the third one until I lightly circled her clit with my tongue.

She made a tortured sound even as she pulsed anew and accepted the third finger.

"Look at how good you are," I said, hoping she couldn't hear my desperation to be inside of her.

She shivered in response and took my fingers deeper.

"Yes, just like that," I said. Then I kissed her clit lightly because it was there and so pretty.

She whimpered and moved her hips on my fingers.

"Do you want more, my sweet Ava?"

"Yes."

The pleading word drove my need to feel her around my cock, but after Allison's story about Hanno hurting her because he went too deep, I was worried about doing the same to Ava. And once I was inside of her, I knew I wouldn't want to stop for a long time. I wanted to stay buried inside of her for the remainder of the day.

"Turn around and brace your hands on the wall."

Some of the haze cleared in her gaze. "Wait...what?"

I withdrew my fingers and kissed her mouth again until she was pliant against me.

"Trust me, Ava. Put your hands on the wall." As I spoke, I guided her hand to the wall, keeping her under the warm water. "Let me see how well your pretty little pussy can take me."

Her cheeks flushed as she slowly turned away from me.

I reached around her, cupping her with one hand. She squeaked when I lifted her, and her hands slid against the wall.

"Uh, I—"

With one arm supporting her waist, I replaced my hand with my cock.

Her moan joined mine as I slowly entered her from behind. Her body squeezed me better than her palm had. The ache in my testicles returned as my fingers found that little nub. I circled around it, coaxing her body to accept more of me.

When her passage started to resist, I gently rolled it between my fingers with very light pressure. She jolted in my arms, bucking even as her pussy relaxed to allow more.

"That's it," I said, my voice strained. "Just like that."

She shivered and tried moving against me. I maintained control of the depth, though, easing her onto me even as my eyes wanted to roll back in my head.

When my hips firmly pressed against her ass, I withdrew and repeated the process several times until her body no longer resisted me. With each pass, the tingling need for release intensified.

"You're so perfect, Ava," I said. "Does anything hurt?"

She shook her head.

"Good."

That was the last word I said before the sound of skin meeting wet skin filled the shower.

I came inside of her three times before she found her second release on my cock. She weakly clung to me as I washed her then carried her to our bed.

Her eyes fluttered open when I kissed her forehead and the tip of her nose.

"My perfect Ava," I said tenderly. "Stay here. Rest. I'll get you something to eat and drink."

I returned with a glass of water and a sandwich. While she ate her sandwich, I feasted on her. She'd tried to tell me I didn't need to, but I proved how much I did. After her third orgasm, I set aside her forgotten sandwich and eased inside of her from the front this time.

"Your pussy feels so good, Ava," I said, watching her face for any signs of discomfort. "Should we see how much it wants to accept?"

It took every inch.

AVA WAS asleep on my chest and drooling on me. I loved it. The sun hadn't yet risen, but the sky was growing lighter. Unfortunately, I knew she wouldn't be ready to wake up for hours yet.

How could I miss her even when she was sleeping on me? I wanted to talk to her, see her smile, hear her laugh, and just enjoy her companionship.

Her soft snores were almost as good, though. Soothing.

I smoothed my hand over the arm she'd slung across my stomach. She sighed in her sleep and snuggled closer, her knee brushing over my cock.

Suppressing a groan, I glanced at the water glass and empty plate waiting on the bedside table. I wanted to stay and cuddle with her until she woke, but I also wanted to have her breakfast ready for her when she opened her eyes. She hadn't eaten much food the day before.

After kissing her forehead, I eased out from under her and went to the kitchen. I knew what Ava really missed eating for breakfast because she'd mentioned it during one of our talking breaks last night. Pancakes. With *real* maple syrup. She'd stressed the "real" part.

I found the pancake mix from the picture on the box. The syrup confused me, though, because I wasn't sure how to tell if it was real or not.

Leaving the house quietly, I jogged to Ryan's house and knocked on the door. Brog answered it after a few moments.

"Is Ryan awake?" I asked.

"Not yet."

"Do you know if this is real?" I held up the bottle.

Brog glanced at it and said, "I'll wake up Ryan."

Ryan shuffled out of his room a few minutes later. "Hey, Gyrik. How are things going with Ava?"

"Good. She showed me her pussy many times yesterday."

"That's great. So, why are you here and not there?"

"She wants real maple syrup. Is this real?" I held out the bottle.

"Nope. That's the fake stuff. I'll take it and trade you for the real stuff. The real stuff usually has a maple leaf on it somewhere." He returned with a different bottle from his kitchen and showed me the leaf. "Some people like the real stuff. Some people prefer the fake stuff. The real savages don't like syrup at all."

Brog looked at me. "I don't like syrup."

I grunted because I'd tasted what was in the bottle before coming over and hadn't liked it either.

Ryan grinned at both of us and handed over the bottle. "Bring Ava over to the red greenhouse as soon as she's done with breakfast. Since she has some seeds, I'll assign her some space she can use."

"I will. Thank you, Ryan."

"Anytime."

I jogged back to the house and had many pancakes made by the time I heard Ava moving in the bedroom. She appeared in the hallway, smoothing down her hair with her hands.

"Good morning, my Ava. Are you sore?" I asked, watching her walk.

"A little."

"I'm sorry. I promise to be more careful today."

She stopped patting her hair and stared at me for a second.

"Um, I'm starting to understand where Allison was coming from yesterday."

My heart clenched in fear.

Ava chuckled and wrapped her arms around my waist.

"I'm still not going to share you. We just might need a few more timeouts today. I didn't realize that your stamina while running also carried over to bedtime fun. Now, what are you making me?"

"Pancakes." I kissed the top of her head and hugged her in return, loving how she felt in my arms. "With real maple syrup."

"You are so perfect, Gyrik."

I smiled widely, glad I'd gone to Ryan's house.

"After you eat, Ryan wants to show you the red greenhouse. He'll assign you an area to use for your grandpa's seeds."

"Perfect."

I stacked two pancakes on a plate for her while she went to the table and pulled one of the seed binders closer to her. As I set her plate and syrup beside her, she opened it and started laughing.

"What is it?"

She pulled a small note from one of the clear pockets that held three seeds.

"It's a note from my grandpa to my mom. It says, 'Don't throw these away this time. Quality seeds are hard to buy.'

"They're marijuana seeds. He even labeled the strain." She shook her head, still smiling. "I hope Ryan's okay with pot plants."

"He'll be okay with anything," I promised her.

EPILOGUE

AVA

THE WARM SUMMER BREEZE MOVED THE HAIR THAT HAD ESCAPED from my sun hat, and I straightened to brush it back from my face as I looked at the rows of chamomile and lavender I'd planted.

It turned out that I didn't just love growing things. I was good at it.

And I was learning so much. Grandpa's notes had gotten me started on the concepts of yield and hardiness, and the books I'd been reading over the past several months only expanded the knowledge.

We now had experimental plant groupings in different fields using a variety of compost mixes.

It was exciting. Fun. Challenging. And I felt like I was a part of something that actually mattered now.

While there were still numerous supply caches in zombie-infested areas that the fey could raid, we all knew they wouldn't last forever. Laying the groundwork for self-sufficiency now would help set us up for success later when the pre-apocalypse provisions ran out.

An engine started, and with a sense of satisfaction, I watched one of the fey move the water tanker closer to the cornfield.

Everyone was preparing for the major harvests we had

planned in the upcoming weeks. The residents in Unity were working hard in the fields. The fey were stockpiling canning supplies, dehydrators, and freeze dryers in Tenacity. Tolerance prepared the prep space and work schedules to preserve everything quickly and efficiently after harvest.

The amount of planning and calculations that had gone into our efforts was staggering. How many people did we need to feed? How much would they need per serving? What did that equate to for plants per field? Did we have enough space? How would we water it all? Did we have room for cattle crops?

The list was endless, but it felt like we had a solid working plan.

Despite staggered plantings, we knew late summer and early fall would be non-stop work. We had corn, carrots, potatoes, green beans, and peas, just to name a few that were growing well. The peas had already seen several harvests. Same with the lettuce.

Fresh produce had never tasted so good. Well, to the humans, anyway. But that didn't stop the fey from pitching in.

I looked at the row of tomatoes and caught Allison waving at me. With a smile, I waved back and watched her pluck a ripe tomato off the vine and bite into it. She gave me a thumbs-up. The small cherry tomatoes were the first things I'd planted in the greenhouse the day after I'd arrived. Pops had saved the seeds, noting they were the sweetest, most tender baby tomatoes he'd ever tasted.

I thought of my family often but hadn't given up hope they were out there.

The groups who searched for survivors were slowly establishing supply drop locations for the people they'd already contacted. We were building better relations with each delivery. However, not everyone was welcoming. People attempted to ambush the supply locations a few times, but they quickly learned that the New Unity trucks weren't easy to overtake.

Allison was still chewing as she pulled her water wagon forward to give the next plant a drink.

Ryan joined me while I was still watching her work.

"It's weird seeing her without Hanno," I said.

"He's never far away." Ryan nodded to a field over where Hanno was following Courtney and Kennedy. Courtney was the first one pregnant in their trio.

"What do you think he'd do if all three were pregnant at once?" I asked.

"Test their patience with his enthusiasm and overprotectiveness."

I grinned and looked at Ryan. "You're pretty smart for eighteen."

"It's not about the years; it's about the experience. And I've had more than my share."

"So, Mr. Experience…what brings you out to the fields?"

"Just got news from Mya that I thought you'd like to hear first instead of through the grapevine."

"Oh?"

"Repeat is a papa, six times over."

"No way."

"Yep. Three girls and three boys. She wants to know if you want to keep any."

I shook my head. "Nah, with all this food we're putting away, we'll want to keep a few for the fields and our food storage."

He nodded.

"Any word from the latest outpost?" I asked.

His happy expression immediately shifted. "Sorry. They showed the picture. No one's seen your family, but it turns out someone recognized a nephew in Tolerance."

Rather than feeling dejected by the news, I felt hopeful. Sharing pictures of the people here in the communities could work. Maybe someday, I would see my family again.

"That's really cool."

"Yep, he's thinking of flying out there to join them. Having a fey-friendly face there for future deliveries will be good.

"In other news, Cassie asked for an update on the home remedy plants."

We started talking about crops and harvests like we always did when we got together. Ryan, despite his youth, was an amazing leader. He actively listened, wanted feedback, and made carefully considered decisions that I rarely disagreed with.

"I think you're right. Greens during winter are going to be important. Easy growers with higher yields make the most sense.

"How are the heirloom strawberry plants growing?"

"We've already doubled what I originally planted, thanks to the runners. I know we need to consider the greenhouse space for winter growth, but I'd really like to keep expanding the patch so we have enough to plant outdoors next year. My backyard has the space, but so does the corner lot on the East side."

"We would have community mutiny if I said no to expanding the strawberry harvest for next spring. The small jars of preserves from this year are already gone. People liked it better than the stuff from the store. Speaking of stores…"

He dug into his pocket and pulled out a baggie with seeds.

"Cassie told Kerr she missed fruit. He raided a grocery store close to here and pulled these out. Apple, orange, and those little ones are bananas. He's not sure they'll grow. The food was pretty rotten."

"I like a challenge," I said. And the idea of growing greenhouse bananas really appealed to me.

Gyrik came running up to us as Ryan passed me the baggie. The big grey dreamsicle I called mine was radiating happiness.

"Did you hear Repeat is a father?" Gyrik asked.

"I did. Did you get to see them?"

Gyrik nodded. "I watched the last one come out. Cat births seem less painful than human births." He seemed to realize what he'd said because he got really quiet.

I patted his arm. "You're not going to scare me, Gyrik. I know how much having a baby will hurt, and no, that won't stop me from wanting to have one with you. It'll happen when it happens."

He nodded and looked off in the direction of Hanno and Courtney.

Gyrik wanted kids bad. Like, *really* bad.

With Mya ready to pop any day now, all the fey were in full baby-daddy mode, captivated by each birth. Cats. Chicks. The cute little bull that was recently born.

They were obsessed.

And that obsession meant we wives lived in the Bone Zone, twenty-four-seven. Bending over to check a roast needed a frying pan ass cover. If not for his fear that I'd start finding sex painful as Allison did, Gyrik would never let me leave the house.

But I knew the moment he found out I was pregnant, I wouldn't leave the house, anyway. Which is why I'd kept it to myself for the last four weeks. But he was a smart man. I'd caught him staring at the tampon supply he'd collected for me.

Ryan caught my eye and indicated that he was going to leave. I nodded and watched him walk away as I waited for Gyrik's attention to return to me.

When it did, I could almost read his thoughts in the way he blinked at me, and I loved the man's sex drive.

"You just had me screaming a few hours ago. We're still on a sex timeout. And, for the record, Childbirth doesn't scare me… having someone tell me I can't do something does."

"I remember," he said. "A dick pushes you down. I'm not a dick."

I grinned at him, loving that he not only remembered my story from when we first met but that he'd obviously asked for an explanation to understand me better. He did that a lot. Quietly asking for guidance so he could be the best version of himself for me.

"Exactly. So, when I get pregnant, what will you want me to do?"

"Anything you want," he said quickly.

"What if I want to help harvest all the fields? It'll make my back sore and my feet hurt. It might even make me too tired for sex. But I'll still want to help with the harvest."

"That's okay. I'll help you when you want it and rub all your sore parts when you're done. Nothing will change. I promise."

He took my hand in his, gently stroking my fingers. The look in his eyes no longer screamed impending visit to Drillville. I saw something else there.

I gave him a considering look.

"You already know, don't you?"

He did the rapid blink morse code thing he did when I busted him on something and he didn't want to admit it. I snorted and tugged my hand from his to wrap my arms around his waist.

"How long have you known?" I asked.

"A while."

"Are you happy?"

"Very."

"Me too. Thank you for finding me, Gyrik. I wouldn't be where I am without you."

I tipped my head back and welcomed his kiss.

AUTHOR'S NOTE

I said I was done with the Resurrection world but so many of you reached out asking for more that I had to listen.

So consider this an epilogue perhaps to the world that ended and maybe a start to a new world if enough people are interested.

If you enjoyed this addition to the Resurrection series (which would really need to be change for any new books if I continue), please leave or review or rating on the retailer of your choice. It let's me know the books are actually being read by someone. ;)

If you want to stay up to date on what I'm writing (or even to vote on what I write next), but sure to subscribe to my newsletter via my website mjhaag.melissahaag.com/subscribe so you can keep up on all my writing news. Since I only send monthly, I won't spam your inbox.

Until next time, happy reading!
Melissa

(If you're looking for more books by me, turn the page!)

THE
RESURRECTION
CHRONICLES

Humor, romance, and sexy dark fey!

Book 1: Demon Ember

In a world going to hell, Mya must learn to accept help from her new-found demon protector in order to find her family as a zombie-like plague spreads.

Book 2: Demon Flames

As hellhounds continue to roam and the zombie plague spreads, Drav leads Mya to the source of her troubles—Ernisi, an underground Atlantis and Drav's home. There Mya learns that the shadowy demons, who've helped devastate her world, are not what they seem.

Book 3: Demon Ash

While in Ernisi, cites were been bombed and burned in an attempt to stop the plague. Now, Marauders, hellhounds, and the infected are doing their best to destroy what's left of the world. It's up to Mya and Drav to save it.

Book 4: Demon Escape

While running from zombies, hellhounds, and the people who kept her prisoner, Eden encounters a new creature. He claims he only wants to protect her. Eden must decide who the real devils are between man and demon, and choosing wrong could cost her life.

Book 5: Demon Deception

Grieving from the loss of her husband and youngest child, Cassie lives in fear of losing her remaining daughter. To gain protection, Cassie knows she needs to sleep with one of the dark fey and give him the one thing she isn't sure she can. Her heart.

THE
RESURRECTION
CHRONICLES

The apocalyptic adventure continues!

BOOK 6: DEMON NIGHT

Angel's growing weaker by the day and needs help. In exchange for food, she agrees to give Shax advice regarding how to win over Hannah. If Angel can help make that happen, just maybe she won't be kicked out when her fellow survivors find out she's pregnant.

BOOK 7: DEMON DAWN

In a post-apocalyptic world, Benna is faced with the choice of trading her body and heart to the dark fey in order to survive the infected.

BOOK 8: DEMON DISGRACE

Hannah is drinking away her life to stanch the bleeding pain from past trauma. Merdon, a dark fey with a violent history, relentlessly sets out to show her there's something worth living for.

BOOK 9: DEMON FALL

June never planned to fall in love. She had her eyes on the prize: a career and independence. Too bad the world ended and stole those options from her. Maybe falling in love had been the better choice after all.

Beauty and the Beast with seductively dark twists!

BOOK 1: DEPRAVITY

When impoverished, beautiful Benella is locked inside the dark and magical estate of the beast, she must bargain for her freedom if she wants to see her family again.

BOOK 2: DECEIT

Safely hidden within the estate's enchanted walls, Benella no longer has time to fear her tormentors. She's too preoccupied trying to determine what makes the beast so beastly. In order to gain her freedom, she must find a way to break the curse, but first, she must help him become a better man while protecting her heart.

BOOK 3: DEVASTATION

Abused and rejected, Benella strives to regain a purpose for her life, and finds herself returning to the last place she ever wanted to see. She must learn when it is right to forgive and when it is time to move on.

TALES
OF
CINDER

Be careful what you wish for...

PREQUEL: DISOWNED

In a world where the measure of a person rarely goes beneath the surface, Margaret Thoning refuses to play by its rules. She walks away from everything she's ever known to risk her heart and her life for the people who matter most.

BOOK 1: DEFIANT

When the sudden death of Eloise's mother points to forbidden magic, Eloise's life quickly goes from fairy tale to nightmare. Kaven, the prince's manservant, is Eloise's prime suspect. However, when dark magic is used, nothing is as simple as it seems.

BOOK 2: DISDAIN

Cursed to silence, Eloise is locked in the tattered remains of her once charming life. The smoldering spark of her anger burns for answers and revenge. However, games of magic can have dire consequences.

BOOK 3: DAMNATION

With the reason behind her mother's death revealed, Eloise must prevent her stepsisters from marrying the prince and exact her revenge. However, a secret of the royal court strikes a blow to her plans. Betrayed, Eloise will question how far she's willing to go for revenge.

TALES OF SNOW

Forbidden fruit never tasted so sweet.

BOOK 1: DESPAIR

To rescue her twin sister from an evil caster, Kellen ventures into the Dark Forest and stumbles upon an enchanted clearing where seven handsome men live. Drawn by their camaraderie and mysterious charm, Kellen must navigate loyalty, longing, and seduction in this captivating reimagining of Snow White.

BOOK 2: DESIRE

As Kellen devotes herself to the forbidden realm of casting to unravel the secrets of the cursed men of the glade, she must confront her innermost desires and step into a world where promises are binding and magic holds the key to freedom.

BOOK 3: DEGRADATION

To save the people she loves and free the imprisoned city, Kellen must forget the rules she's learned and embrace who she is destined to be—a power to overcome the greatest evil she's ever known.